Because of a Bee

Because, Volume 1

Elle White

Published by Elle White, 2026.

This is a work of fiction. Similarities to real people, places, or events are entirely coincidental.

BECAUSE OF A BEE

First edition. March 13, 2026.

ISBN: 979-8994471715

Written by Elle White.

For David, the light that always shines to bring me home.

Chapter 1

Ryan

If I had known I would be meeting the man I had a crush on in high school while stripping on the side of the road, I would have stayed in bed.

I rolled over and looked at the clock; it was time to get up. I knocked the book I had been reading the night before onto the floor. Late-night reading was beginning to take its toll on my ability to get up in the morning.

Everything in my grandmother's house was analog. She had tried to keep everything the same after my grandfather died. When I moved back into the house, I didn't want to make any changes. Some of the things were new; I brought all the things I'd collected in college. Otherwise, I was surrounded by the things I'd grown up with.

When the time finally registered in my brain, I fell out of bed in my hurry to get up. That should have been the first sign that I should get back in and stay there. The entire morning was turning into a comedy of errors. The hot water didn't come on. At the end of what was becoming a very fast shower, the hot water finally came on. Since I had it turned up, I nearly scalded myself trying to get it to shut off. I forgot to buy my favorite cereal the day before and had to find something else.

I don't do well with change.

The lack of cereal became a lack of breakfast. I decided my usual routine of going to the Coffee Shop for a cup of cocoa before work would also provide breakfast.

The next mishap came as I ripped the zipper on my skirt. Which meant that on the day I usually wear a skirt, I needed to wear pants. Grabbing my favorite pants out of the closet. They weren't jeans, which are against the dress code except on Saturdays, but they were similar. Finally dressed, I grabbed my backpack.

My car, which had been my grandmother's, decided not to start. The thing was over twenty years old and barely held together. I knew I would need to replace it soon. I keep putting it off. It's a part of my grandmother that I can't let go of.

Doing what I always do in times of crisis with my car, I called my uncle. "Hey, Good morning."

"Good morning. I am going to assume that this call is about your car not starting."

"You are a mind reader." I quickly pulled all my things out of the car. I grabbed the helmet off the shelf and got my motorcycle ready.

"I'll come by and look at it later this morning. I haven't even had my coffee. Or my breakfast." There was a pause. I knew what he was going to say before he said it. "You know you are going to have to replace it, right. That car is not going to keep going forever." He was using his patient voice. The one he used when he knew I wasn't going to a, like what he was going to say, and b, want to do whatever it was he was going to suggest.

"I know. I'm not ready."

"Are you ever going to be ready?" His voice gentled even more. "At some point in time, you are going to have to let go of the physical things and keep the memories."

"I know, okay, I know," my voice was close to breaking. So many things were not working out this morning, and I was one more thing away from a full meltdown. The fact that I had only had a few hours of sleep thanks to the book I read last night wasn't helping.

"I'll come by and look at it later this morning and let you know what I find. You should probably consider looking for another car."

"Thanks. I'll take the bike to work this morning. The weather is supposed to be good all day." I didn't ride when there was a chance of rain. Other people had no problem. I might have been riding for the last nine years, but I was not a fan of riding in the rain.

Spring could be tricky. It could be warm or cold. I grabbed my leather jacket off the hook by the door. I used it for warmth and protection in case of an accident. I backed the bike out of the garage. After making sure everything was locked down and where it needed to be, I started it up.

The sun felt great. The breeze felt great. Everything felt great. The morning was going to be great. That was way too many greats and should have warned me that things were going to change.

I felt a flutter at the top of my jacket. Then it moved down into my clothes. I had experienced this once before. That time had not ended well, and I did not want a repeat of the experience.

I tried to stay calm as I made the curve and saw the pull-off on the right. It had once been a rest stop for people traveling along the back roads before they put the highway in. The tables were gone, but the area was still used by people wanting to look out at the lake on the other side of the trees. In the summer, people would come and swim at the little beach. The town gave up the fight to keep people from using the area as a beach and put portable toilets in.

All that was far from my mind as I pulled into the parking area.

Before I had even gotten the kick stand down, I was pulling off my jacket. I let it fall behind me on the seat. Followed by my shirt. I was seriously hoping the bee would fly off before I had to take off my tank top. Sitting in public in only my bra was not at the top of my list of things to do.

I felt the bee fly off from my skin just as I heard the sound of a car door shutting behind me. The small reprieve that I had experienced in all my "great" moments was rapidly turning my morning into a nightmare. I turned and looked over my shoulder.

Yup, someone was getting out of their car and heading my way. The position of my head was not conducive to seeing who was walking towards me, and I felt very vulnerable in my tank top. I grabbed my shirt and started to put it back on.

"Are you okay? I saw you weave a little before pulling off, and I wanted to make sure you were okay."

The voice was nice. Not too deep and a little rough. It had that "I just woke up and am not used to talking yet" kind of feel.

"I'm fine. A bee flew into my clothes." I turned more fully once I had my shirt on and buttoned. He had stopped at the side of his car, staying far enough away that I felt a little safer talking with him. He wasn't encroaching on my space.

"Are you okay? Sorry, I already asked that. Did you get stung?"

"No, I'm fine. It got free before it stung me."

"How have you been, Ryan?"

I looked at him more closely. Then it hit me. This was a grown-up version of the boy I had had a crush on in high school. It wasn't much of a crush. Mostly the "from a distance I worship you" kind of crush. I didn't date in high school. I wanted to date in high school. But two things kept me from doing that: my intense social anxiety and awkwardness.

I dated in college, and then also when I moved back to work at the library. But those dates always ended in awkward situations or awkward conversations. Neither of which fills me with any type of positive feelings. My best friend Annie says that when I find the right person, I will feel safe enough to be myself. I have yet to prove that statement correct. Probably because, as she says, I haven't met the right person.

"Braden," I couldn't help the breathy way I said his name. It just came out that way. "I'm good. Well, except for the bee incident." I picked up my jacket and put it back on. "I didn't know you were back."

"I teach at the high school."

"Oh, that's great. Um, I really need to get going. I have a meeting." I started the bike back up and put my helmet on. "It was good seeing you." With that, I rode off in a cloud of social anxiety and embarrassment. Nothing like stripping on the side of the road and then seeing someone from your past. If I'm lucky, this will be a one-and-done thing, and I will never have to think about stripping on the side of the road right before seeing someone from my past ever again.

I have never been that lucky.

I pulled into the back parking lot of the library. We shared the lot with the church next door. They didn't have a lot going on during the week, and we didn't have anything going on Sunday. It worked out well for both groups. The church did a lot for the people in the community. I know this because my aunt is a member of the congregation. I went with her every Sunday while I lived with them. I hadn't been in a while. Something my aunt reminded me I needed to fix.

I waved at Patty as she headed in the back door. She was the secretary to the pastor. I had heard that there was an interim pastor for a few months while the regular one was healing up from a health scare. My aunt probably had all the information. I'd never asked.

The walk to the Coffee Shop took only a few minutes. I walked past the bookstore and pharmacy. I loved looking at the bookstore window. The owner, Florie, was part of the book group. Her daughter Michelle ran the shop when Florie went to Book Club meetings. Michelle had graduated with a degree in marketing, and since she went to work for Florie, the shop had started to grow and draw in new customers. The window displays were always worth looking at. The current display featured a new book by Florie's nephew. His mysteries sell well. There was a long waiting list at the library for his new book. Annie loved them. He's one of her favorite authors. I know this because every time someone checks out or returns one of his books, she says it.

I always look in the window before going into the Coffee Shop. When Connie took over, she didn't want to keep calling it Rosie's because she was not Rosie. Rosie was her aunt. Connie took over the place when her aunt retired. We had taken a poll, and Coffee Shop was what we came up with. Catchy, and you knew exactly what you were there for. Well, not me, I don't drink coffee. I drink peppermint tea or cocoa. In the summer, Connie makes a killer iced cocoa.

There were a lot of people in line, but not as many of them sat at the tables. My usual table was free. Opening the door, I scurried past the people standing in line and put my things down at my table. Sliding into my usual seat, I looked out at the rest of the customers. Safely tucked into the back corner with a view of everything, I still missed my cousin Jared moving in on me.

I had placed my large bag on the floor and was leaning down to get my e-reader out when I heard the chair across from me scrape. I looked up into the smiling face of my cousin.

"Good morning," he said. He leaned on the chair instead of sitting, motioning to someone I couldn't see from my seated position. "You are officially the most interesting thing in town this morning." He moved the chair towards me, making room for more chairs.

"What are you talking about?" I asked even though I knew exactly where this was going. My luck had well and truly run out for the day.

"Everyone wants to know why you were seen stripping off your clothes with a man on the side of the road this morning?"

"Is Jason coming?"

"What?"

"Jason, your brother, remember him? I am only going to tell this story one time."

"You just *think* you're going to tell this story one time. Everyone is going to want to hear about this. Aren't you working at the desk this morning?"

"How do you know I'm working at the desk?"

"Because," He paused while his brother Jason pulled a chair over from another table. Then, looking me in the eye, said, "We already talked to Annie and she told us that if we didn't see you here, you would be working at the desk."

"Did she tell you?" Jason looked so much like his brother that people who didn't know them thought they were twins. They weren't. Jared was older by one year. Jason had been a surprise. The two of them were inseparable. I knew that because I grew up with them. Jason and I were in the same grade in school. Women of all ages found them irresistible once they turned on their charm. Maybe it was the combination of dark hair and blue eyes. I knew they were handsome. I also knew I didn't need to tell them that.

"No, she didn't tell me. We were waiting for you."

Turning to respond to him, I noticed Connie moving towards us. She had cocoa and a muffin. Which I hoped was for me.

"Did you tell them yet?"

"No, Connie. We were waiting for you," Jared said.

"Oh, good. Here, these are for you." She placed the treats in front of me and then grabbed another chair to squeeze up to our table. "Move over, Jared."

"Where exactly am I supposed to move to? I could sit in Jason's lap." His sarcasm was lost on Connie. Or at least it seemed to be until she responded with a devilish smile.

"Oh, could you? That would be so helpful."

"I am only going to tell this tale one time," I said.

"She thinks," Jason muttered to his brother.

"That's what I told her."

"Guys, enough. This is what happened." I launched into the tale of the car not starting and taking the bike, and I was able to talk undisturbed until I got to the part where Braden pulled over to help.

"Braden from high school," Jared asked. "The one that had a crush on you?"

"He did not have a crush on me. I was invisible in high school. No one paid attention to me." Jared and Jason looked at each other for a long minute and then turned back to me. "What? Why are you two looking at each other like that?"

"Nothing." It was suspicious that they both responded at the same time. Also suspicious that they didn't actually answer the question.

"As I said, nothing happened."

"That is the least dramatic retelling of a potentially gossip-worthy story I have ever heard. I expected better from you." Connie stood up and looked over at the counter. "I have to go help out. I expect more from you later," she pointed at me as she spoke.

"She's right. That was a complete let-down. You need to work on your delivery," Jason said as he stood up, returning the chairs to the table behind him, smiling at the woman seated there.

"We need to get going. You do realize that there's going to be a lot of questions about your adventure?" Jared nudged his brother to get his attention. "Say goodbye."

"What?" Jason looked over at me with the flirtatious smile on his face that he had been directing at the poor woman sitting next to us. "Oh, bye. Are you going to the family cookout?"

"Yes," I said to him. Then, turning to the woman, Fran, at the other table, "Are you and the twins coming to the children's hour later?"

"Oh, definitely. I escaped this morning. My mother is visiting and is looking after the boys."

I watched as a look of horror crossed over Jason's face as he glanced back at Fran. That man would flirt with anyone but was absolutely terrified of responsibility.

"Let's go, Romeo." Jared punched his brother's arm and led him away. He waved at me on his way out the door.

"That man is a serious flirt." Fran was laughing as she watched them go out the door.

"That he is. That he is."

Chapter 2

Braden

I couldn't help but stare after her as she rode off. When I got out of bed this morning, the last thing I thought I would see on my way to work was Ryan. I hadn't seen her since graduation day. I'd thought about her a lot over the years. The one thing I never thought was that I'd be driving down the road and see her at the pull-off stripping off her clothes.

The rest of my ride to work was filled with memories of high school, which seemed semi-fitting since that same high school was where I was going now. There was a lot to unpack from those few minutes with Ryan.

I sat in the car outside the high school for a few minutes, trying to process my morning thus far. I had tried to leave early, only to have to change a tire. I got behind a motorcycle and thought about a girl I'd had a crush on in high school. I watched as the rider started moving erratically on the road, only to pull off and start removing her clothes. I know I said that part already; I cannot emphasize enough the shock of seeing Ryan removing her shirt on the side of the road.

As I got out of my car at the school, I realized my shirt was untucked. As teachers, we were supposed to dress a certain way. I struggled with it every single day. I hated tucking my shirt in. I settled for the fashionable half-tucked thing a friend had shown me. It might not be within the bounds of dress code, but it was as far as I was willing to go.

Entering the building, I moved into stealth mode. My goal was to get past the secretary's office without being seen. While everyone knows that the secretary knows everything, in our school, she and the principal have worked together for so long that they basically share power. Though she is the secretary in title, she seems to have more control than the vice principal. And her door is always open. Not in the friendly way that encourages people to come and talk. It is more like, "My door is open, and I'm watching you."

I made it into my classroom without being seen. The students had a three-day weekend. We didn't. I needed to be at the school for meetings and to attend professional development workshops. No one took any sort of attendance, so, depending on the subject of the presentation, I would usually hide in my room. One of the things I want to check on for the students is whether the library has the display of books I requested up and ready. A few weeks earlier, I'd talked to the head librarian, a man named Frank. He said it would be no problem, but that was the last I heard from him.

I barely sat down at my desk when the door opened. It opened as slowly and as quietly as possible. If I were lucky, it would be one of the other teachers. If I were unlucky, it would be the principal or her secretary trying to sneak up on me. Both of them were watching me, I was told. It wasn't like I did anything memorable as a student. I'd kept my head down and gotten good grades. My sister, on the other hand, had been, shall I say, memorable. Now that I was a teacher, they were watching for signs of rebellion and unrest; I had been told this by a reliable source—the janitor.

As the door finished opening, I could see who it was. They faced the hallway, backing into the room. As they cleared the door, they closed it quietly, still trying to see into the hall till the last possible second before the door finally closed.

"Stan, what are you doing?"

His startle reflex is legendary. It didn't matter how gentle, quiet, or obvious you were. If he didn't see you and you said something, he jumped. His students took advantage of this without mercy.

"Oh, good, you're here. The others will be here soon. We're trying not to raise suspicion with you know who." I did know who.

A few minutes later, the door opened again, and two more teachers slid into the room—Lydia and Brian. They had barely started as teachers when I graduated. I was in Lydia's class as a senior. It was weird at the time to have a teacher who was only five years older than their students. I talked to Brian a lot about becoming a teacher. They were as excited as I was when I got the job teaching English. There were quite a few teachers still teaching whom I had had as a student. Most of them were friendly and talked to me as colleagues. Others looked at me with wariness, seeing me as the teen they knew rather than as an adult.

"Are you ready for the influx tomorrow?" Lydia said.

"Why do they do this? Why do we have a vacation, come back, and then get a three-day weekend?" Brian hated any break in his scheduled life. However, to be fair to the school, this was on the calendar and not a surprise.

"Brian, who cares?" She turned her attention towards me, "The real question is, what were you doing at the overlook this morning?" Lydia waggled her eyebrows at me.

"I stopped to help someone." I tried to leave it at that, but Lydia was giving me her teacher look. The one that said, *I know there is more, and I am waiting*. I still had not mastered the look. "She had a bee fly down her shirt while riding into work this morning. I stopped to make sure she was okay."

"Do you know who she is," Brian asked as he tried to maneuver himself into a desk.

Lydia grabbed his arm and directed him toward a chair next to her. "Stop before you hurt yourself. Just sit here."

"It was Ryan Matthewson."

"Oh, the librarian. I talk to her about new books sometimes. She always has a good recommendation. Do you know her?" Stan maneuvered his chair so he could see the door and still talk with us. He and the secretary had a very disagreeable exchange and had yet to recover from it. Now he lived in constant fear of her.

"Didn't she graduate with you?" Lydia had her phone out, tapping at it.

"Yes. I knew her cousin."

"Is that it? By the way your eyes lit up when you said her name, I thought you were going to say that you two had been in love in high school."

"My eyes did not light up."

"Oh yes, they did. Didn't they, Brian? Stan?"

"I thought they did a little." Stan was now peering into my eyes as though he was trying to see into my brain.

"I wasn't looking." Brian was busy trying to see what Lydia was doing on her phone.

"Fine. I know what I saw. There is a story there." She motioned at me with a hurry up gesture. "Tell us. Quick, before we get caught." Lydia glanced at Stan, who was still watching the door as if he knew it was going to be thrown open at any moment by the school secretary.

Everyone was staring at me, waiting for me to speak. It was very disconcerting.

"There isn't much to tell. I always liked her, but I was too shy to ask her out. And her cousins made sure that everyone stayed away from her. Not in any aggressive way. I think she was shy, and they were very protective. On the first day of our junior year, she showed up to school riding a motorcycle."

There was way more to the story than that. I wasn't sure if I wanted to share it with them yet. I remember her showing up on her motorcycle as if it were an everyday event. Which, for her, it probably was. But, for us mere mortal males, it was as though a goddess had descended. She parked her bike, took off her helmet, and shook her hair. Not in that Hollywood way where the camera slows down, and the light catches it. She just reached up and pulled her hair out of the back of her sweatshirt. It could have been like the Hollywood version for how much it inspired me. Unfortunately, she also caught the attention of every other male in the parking lot.

She walked past me on her way into the building, smiling at me. I can see it even now. That morning made a huge impression on me. Not as big an impression as her cousins did when they glared at every boy watching her, however.

I also noticed the high school queen bee staring at her—and not in a nice way.

"Don't you have something going on at the library," Brian said, interrupting my thoughts.

Stan was moving towards the door. He was almost there when it suddenly opened, and he screamed. I never heard a grown man hit that high a note before in my life. He fell back against a desk, clutching his heart.

"What are the four of you doing? I thought you would be on your way to the auditorium for the faculty meeting." Mrs. Tussle, The Secretary, had found us.

I am sure she has an official title that sounds way better than The Secretary. But not one that would fit her better.

"We were just trying to work out our thoughts on a group project." Lydia was moving quickly towards the door as she spoke over her shoulder. She had Brian by the arm and was shooing Stan out ahead of her.

"You all teach different subjects. What could you possibly do together?" She stared at me, the only remaining victim. If this were a horror movie, I'd be the first one dead after that abandonment.

"We are trying to look at a cross-section of learning involving the liberal arts and sciences. We are just starting to come up with parameters." I smiled my most sincere smile at her as I gathered what I needed for the meeting—mostly my phone and a notebook. The notebook was used to track how many times the principal said the word fluid. We weren't sure how she managed to say that word in so many sentences and still have them make sense, which is why we kept track. Everyone would guess how many times she'd say it, and the winner who came closest would get a point. At the end of the semester, the person with the lowest number of points bought breakfast for our first morning meeting of each semester.

I continued to smile at her as I tried to scurry past. "You were such a quiet boy. The older you get, the more you remind me of your sister." She paused before adding, "That is not a compliment."

She somehow managed to get out the door before me. I sighed as I shut off the light. It was going to be a long day. Then I remembered. Ryan worked at the library, and I would need to go down there to check on the book display. And the day suddenly seemed a lot brighter.

Chapter 3

Ryan

Annie waited for me outside the library. She leaned on the door, watching me. She'd known exactly where I would be before work, which meant she knew it would be impossible to talk to me. Which is why I found her outside the library door. She didn't want me to get away.

She wore her usual work clothes— casual pants and a button-down shirt. Her red hair was loose, falling almost to her waist; she'd have it up before the library opened. I used to braid her hair in high school because I could do it tighter than she could, and she hated having it loose and floating around her face. Now, she just let it do what it wanted.

"Well," was all she said. She propped her hand on her hip for emphasis.

"What?"

"What do you mean, what?"

"What," I repeated.

"You never make anything easy," she sighed. "What happened this morning? And who is the guy you are allegedly having a flaming affair with and secretly meeting at the lookout?"

"There is so much wrong with that," I said as I stopped next to her. "One, why would I meet someone, and I cannot stress the total craziness of this thought, secretly, at one of the most viewed places in town? And two, how could I be having an affair and you not know about it? I can't even add to my secret stash of chocolate at my own house without you knowing about it."

"Okay, I see your point." Annie barely managed to unlock the door. The lock mechanism was always stuck; it was our main complaint to the maintenance people. After three years, we'd given up hope of anyone fixing it.

One of the regular patrons, who always tried to sneak in before we were open, tried to come in with us.

"Not today; we have things that need to be done." Annie closed the door before they could reach the top step.

"Wow, I have never seen you shut someone out before."

"There is no way I want to ask my questions if there is an audience. I want the real answers, not the ones you give to nosy people."

"What about Mabel? She is probably already here."

"Mabel is in the children's section prepping for the incoming horde of preschoolers. And if she comes out, you know she will get the information out of you, and it's not like everyone else isn't going to be asking you about it. I want the real unfettered truth. Not the watered-down version you give to people who are not your best friend."

We both knew that the questioners would be relentless and would frame the questions in the most politely nosy way possible. And that I would give the least salacious and sometimes most boring answers.

I tossed my bag in the bottom drawer of my desk. I watched as Annie carefully placed her large bag in her drawer. She once tried to toss her bag like I did and crushed all the cookies she kept hidden in there for emergencies. She never tried again.

"Well, spill!"Annie had lost all semblance of patience.

"I was riding into work this morning, and a bee flew into my clothes. Or, more likely, I rode into the bee, and it landed in my clothes. They were burrowing down, so I quickly pulled over to get them out. I didn't want to get stung again. I started taking everything off so they could fly off. Luckily, I only had to go down to the tank top."

"And the guy?"

"The guy was someone who pulled over to see if I needed help. That's the whole story."

"Who was he?"

"What do you mean?"

"You know what I mean. Who was he?"

"It was Braden Mitchel."

Annie scrunched her forehead in thought. A slow smile spread over her mouth as she stood up from her desk and walked toward the shelves.

I started getting things set up at the desk. I was turning on the computer when Annie came back with a yearbook.

"I thought so," she said.

"What?" I tried to look as though I wasn't interested, which I totally was.

I tried to take the yearbook from her. She closed it before I could get it away from her. Fortunately, an index listed all the pages on which you could find the person. And there he was. He was listed as being in the writing club, the journalism group, and the track team. He was pretty busy, just as I remembered him

There was a knock at the front door. I looked up and noticed we were a few minutes late opening. The preschool group was probably waiting outside.

Annie rushed over to unlock the door, again struggling with the lock. The first moms and little ones went past. Some of the moms smiled, and some looked like they wanted to stop and chat. As I watched them walk by, I was so thankful for the children with them, pulling them along in their wake.

I watched one of the little girls lead her mom off while telling her about what story she hoped they would be reading. As I turned to go toward my desk, I heard a slight knock on the counter. I turned to look and, not seeing anyone, looked down. Standing at the desk was a small dinosaur. I could only see the top of their head, but I recognized a dinosaur when I saw one.

I leaned over the counter to say hello.

"Hi, how are you today?"

A face I had seen almost every preschool day was smiling at me from the open mouth of the dinosaur head.

"Hi! Will you be my girlfriend?"

I looked up at his aunt, who was standing behind him in time to see her roll her eyes. I smiled at her before I spoke to the little guy.

"Don't you think I might be a little bit too old for you?"

He blew air out of his nose in a remarkable snort for someone so small. "Maybe another day." He turned and headed off. Originally, I had thought the woman with him was his mom. Annie had straightened me out about that. She was his aunt. His mother had passed away a few years before leaving him in his aunt's care.

She mouthed, "Sorry," to me as they went.

"That boy is going to be something when he gets to high school," Annie said.

"High School? I was thinking of Kindergarten. I'm surprised there isn't a trail of broken hearts behind him. But now..."

"But now?"

"He doesn't seem the type."

"How can you tell? He's four."

"I don't know. Just a feeling."

We both turned as the door flew open. A large group of people came into the library almost simultaneously. A few got stuck in the opening for a moment before straightening themselves out. If the door had been wider, they would probably have made it. Some of them went to the book stacks, and others made their way toward me.

"Ryan, dear, are you all right? I heard about this morning." One of our older patrons positioned herself in front of me. Her friends stood nearby to listen, but not close enough to look like they were listening.

The onslaught of questions had begun, and I only had eight more hours to go.

Frank, our head librarian, had left for his vacation the previous Friday. This was the first day I was officially in charge of the library.

I didn't remember Frank being this busy. To be honest, I was usually too busy to notice what he was doing. I just never thought he had very much to do. He always looked like he was one yawn away from a nap at his desk. I gave up trying to get his work and my work done. I finally closed myself in his office. I shut the door so that I could deal with some of the issues that had come up without the constant interruptions from the desk.

I finished the report for the broken sink in the bathroom; the maintenance people wanted detailed reports before they would fix anything. I was so engrossed in what I was doing that the knock on the door startled me.

"Hey," Annie said, putting her head in the door. "There is a call for Frank about a book display for an English teacher up at the school." Annie was smiling at me in a way that made me nervous.

"Okay, I'll get it here." I reached over to the phone and hit the flashing button.

"Hello, Ryan Matthewson. Can I help you?"

"Hello, this is Braden Mitchell."

That was why she had looked at me funny. The man I was supposed to be having a torrid romance with was on the phone.

"How can I help you?" All business. That was me. It didn't matter that he had a fantastic voice. I am not going to melt, I told myself.

"I was wondering how the display was going. I didn't hear back from the man I spoke to, and I was hoping everything was going okay."

"What display?" I began to rifle through the papers Frank had stacked on his desk. Somewhere in this mess must be something about books for display.

"Oh, um, I talked to him last week about a display of books for my students to choose from for a reading project. I'm trying to get them to read more, well, some of them, others I can't keep their nose out of a book long enough to get their homework done. Not that there are very many of the second group, really only one or two. But still, I wanted to give them a choice in books."

"When did you need the display up for?"

"Tomorrow?" It sounded more like a question than an answer.

"Tomorrow? I am not sure I can do that. I don't know where Frank put the list of books. Did you give him a hard copy of the list?"

"Yes, I gave it to him when I came in to talk to him last week." That must have been on my day off, which was probably why I didn't know anything about the display.

"I can't find it on his desk. Do you have another copy you could email me?"

"Oh, no need for that. I'll run it right down."

The phone disconnected before I could say anything. It seemed like I was going to see Braden Mitchel again.

Chapter 4

Ryan

I peeked out of Frank's office to check on Annie. A few people were hovering by the desk. When they saw me, they all waved, trying to get my attention. I knew exactly why they wanted me to come closer, and I was not going.

"Annie, someone's coming by in a few minutes to meet with me. Can you let me know when they show up?"

"Sure. Anyone I know?" She winked at me before turning back around to face the people at the desk.

"Funny." I went back into the office.

I continued to look around Frank's desk for any notes about the display. Knowing him, he probably forgot in his hurry to get out the door on vacation. It had been a hard year for his family, and he needed that vacation. I gave up and sat down as Annie knocked on the door and opened it for Braden to enter.

"I'll be out here if you need anything." Again, she winked at me. Braden happened to look at her as she did it. The need to crawl under my desk was overwhelming.

Gesturing to Annie, Braden asked, "What was that about?"

"I have no idea." I probably could have sounded more long-suffering if I tried harder.

"I brought the list with me. I was hoping to get the display up so we could start this week. Is that possible? I mean, maybe not tomorrow, but in the next couple of days?"

I took the list from him as he sat down. I had been dreading a list filled with books that we didn't have. Looking at the list, I noticed that it was pretty doable. There were a few that had been checked out recently; otherwise, I had either shelved or recently seen most of them. I noticed a glaring, well, glaring to me, omission from the list.

"You don't have any graphic novels."

"I only want real books."

That was like waving a red flag at me. I've helped so many young readers start on a path toward a greater love of reading through graphic novels. There had even been a couple of reluctant readers who struggled with learning to read, who made connections with the graphic novels. Reading those books had helped them become proficient in reading.

"Graphic novels are books. Thus, the name, novels."

Braden put his hands up in defense, and I realized I may have been a little harsh. "I have always seen them as just glorified comic books," he said.

"What's wrong with comic books?"

"Okay, I can see that I have made a misstep."

"Braden, I have teens and young readers, as well as some adults, come in here all the time looking for graphic novels. Some of them come because they love the genre, as do I, and some come because it is an easier format for them to focus on. Some don't have the focus for a novel or the desire to read a novel-length book. They do, however, have the desire to read a graphic novel. Have you read any before? If you let me, I can add a few graphic novels to your list that would fit the types of stories you are trying to get them to read. Only a couple. You may find that some of your students who would otherwise try to avoid this assignment might enjoy it."

"These are high school kids."

"I graduated from college and just finished reading one last night. What's your point?"

He stared at me for a minute. Trying to judge my responses. "I can see this is a hill you would die on and a battle I am wise enough to avoid. Please put a few on the list."

"I'm sorry. You're right. It is a hill I would die on. I love books, and I love to read. Sometimes, I think there is too much pressure on people to read what others think they should read instead of what might bring them joy or interest." I looked around the room, knowing I had some books in my bag to take home. I found my tote bag by the door. I handed Braden a recent fantasy graphic novel that I had just checked in and then checked out for myself that morning.

"Here, try this. Let me know what you think." As I handed it to him, I thought maybe fantasy wasn't his favorite genre. "Is the genre okay? We have a lot in other genres."

"No. The book is fine." He had opened it and was looking through the pages.

"I can probably get these pulled today." I had gone back to looking at the list. "Finding a spot and setting up the display might take some time. But I should have it ready by the time school lets out tomorrow."

I looked down at the list and thought about the display. When Braden spoke, I jumped and pushed my chair back.

"Oh, sorry. I didn't mean to startle you."

"My fault. I sometimes forget other things are going on around me when I am focusing. What were you saying?"

"I said if you think of anything else to put on it to fill out the list, please do."

I could hear a disturbance at the desk through the door. Before I reached the door, Annie opened it and held the knob while she talked to someone outside.

"Frank is not here today. You can leave a message with me or send him an email. He'll get back to you when he returns."

"Well, who is in the office then? Whoever is in the office is in charge, and this needs to be taken care of right now."

I knew that voice. It was a voice I lived in dread of hearing. Tammy came in every Monday like clockwork. To check out a book or to just harass me. I had no idea why she felt the need to continue bullying me long after high school. I thought that people grew out of their teenage habits, like bullying the quiet girl from school.

Tammy had always been there like water torture. Slowly dripping her comments on me, eroding my self-confidence and self-esteem. My therapist helped me with some of it when I went away to college. And when there was no threat of seeing her, things went well; the social anxiety that I experienced had eased. When I returned and started at the library, Tammy seemed to find new reasons to come into the library, and while she was there, she would drip venom in my direction. She rarely bothered Annie, and she drove Frank to tears with her complaints. The fact that I was not out in the public eye for her to torment meant she needed to find someone else. And that someone else was whoever was in the office.

As she pushed through the door, Braden reached over to take the list from me. He had his pen out, so I could only assume he was adding something to the list. It looked to anyone coming in the door as though he were reaching for my hand—as in wanting to hold my hand—which, I am not going to lie, would have been very helpful with the amount of anxiety I was ratcheting up.

"Oh, isn't this sweet? Frank is away, so you hide in his office to meet with men. I'm sure Frank will want to know about that. As will the library board."

"Can I help you, Tammy?" I tried to sound calm. By the look in her eye, I guess I didn't quite make it.

She leaned against the door frame and smiled, her small, tight smile—the one she always wore when she thought she was going to win at one of her little games.

Braden looked at me and raised one of his eyebrows. He looked at my face, which I knew was starting to show signs of the strain of holding in my rising anxiety. He gathered his things and turned to Tammy.

"Tammy, I didn't realize you were still around. I thought someone said you had gotten married and moved away." Braden stood but didn't try to shake hands or make any move toward her.

Tammy, however, once she realized who it was, went toward Braden, intending to hug him. Before she could quite get there, he bent down to pick up the bag he had placed on the floor. As he stood up, he turned towards me.

"Thanks for your help with the list. If there is any problem with the books, I put my email at the bottom of the page." He tapped on the paper. When I looked, I noticed that not only his email but also his phone number was there.

"Of course. We should have the books up by tomorrow. I'll let you know if there is a problem."

As he moved past, he used his shoulder to herd Tammy out the door. He started asking her questions as he went, giving her no other choice but to follow him if she wanted to be heard. She had started preening the moment he started talking.

I watched them go. As I moved toward the office door, Annie signaled me to go back. I took her advice and went back to the desk. I kept the door open; I needed to hear the sounds of people moving. I needed to know I wasn't alone and that help was nearby.

The anxiety that had started when I heard Tammy's voice was beginning to recede. I was sitting with my eyes closed and doing my timed breathing. I heard Annie say she would show someone where to find their book. I started easing back and opening my eyes when I heard the door close.

I opened my eyes fully and saw Tammy standing in front of the closed door.

"Well, wasn't that cozy?" She moved toward the chair and sat. I stayed silent, waiting for her to say whatever it was that she needed to say.

I just sat silently watching her, trying to blank my expression. Maybe if I gave her nothing to work with, as my therapist once said, she'd go away. That wasn't really what my therapist said, but it was how I interpreted it. We sat there, me not saying anything with a blank look, and Tammy slowly building up to a good seethe.

"You're way out of his league. I hope you don't think he'll ask you out."

"Is there anything library-related I can help you with?" I said it with as little emotion as I could. I was not going to let her into my head. Well, any more than she already was.

"Yes, I want to know why I wasn't called when the new book I have been waiting for came in—the new mystery by that woman's nephew—the woman in that ridiculous book club. Anyway, I saw someone else leave with the book. I know I was supposed to be called."

I turned toward the computer and looked up the book. The new system lets me see the waiting list for all the books on hold. Many times, people would hear about a book and then ask to be put on a waiting list, even if we weren't sure we were getting it. Frank used the list as a guide when he ordered books.

As I suspected, Tammy's name was below some others. As I looked at her, I realized that she already knew this. She was looking for any reason to complain about something. I wouldn't put it past her to realize that I was in charge of the library. It was a bonus for her—a reason to complain, and she got to make my life difficult.

She could only make my day as miserable as I let her. I knew that in my brain, but somewhere between knowing it and making it happen, the thought took a left turn and went somewhere else. I continued with my no-expression face, mainly because it seemed to bother her, and I was not above feeling some satisfaction in that.

"You are on the list. But, there are several names ahead of yours."

"Well, fix that. I need to read the book next. My mother read it and wants to talk to me about it. But I won't let her until I read it, and she is getting impatient. At this rate, she will have forgotten the book by the time I get it."

"I'm sorry—" I wasn't sorry. I shrugged my shoulders. "You'll have to wait in line like everyone else. Sometimes, we get a second copy, but I don't think that's going to happen." Was I happy that I had given her bad news? Yes. It gave me no end of joy not to give her what she wanted. I would feel bad about that later.

"Frank would put me up on the list."

I knew very well that Frank would not put her name higher on the list. His wife was the next person on the list, and there was no way he would want to hear about that at home.

"I'm sorry, but that's the rule. Have you read the other books by that author? I'm sure we have something from his backlist."

Tammy just glared at me while I sat there with a pleasant smile. I was proud of myself for staying strong, but I also knew that the panic attack I was actively trying to tamp down was going to be a big one.

"Fine." Tammy got up from her chair, glaring at me for a full minute before turning and leaving the office. She made sure to slam the door on her way out.

I waited to see if she was coming back. With her, you never know what's going to happen. When she didn't, I put my head down. Whatever they cleaned the desk with was making my forehead stick to it.

"Are you okay?"

I was so busy trying to regulate my breathing and not hyperventilate that I didn't hear Annie open the door. I lifted my hand and gave her a thumbs-up in response. There was no way I was going to be able to talk for a few more minutes.

"Okay then. Let me know if you need me." I heard the door close softly.

The day just kept getting better and better.

Chapter 5

Ryan

The day could have been better, but it also could have been worse. I could have had a full-scale meltdown after encountering Tammy, but I didn't. I will take that as a win. My therapist would be so proud.

Since I had my motorcycle, I was limited in what I could grab to bring home to ease my battered spirit. Luckily, my freezer already contained several cartons of ice cream. Trying to bring ice cream home in my backpack once led to me getting a new backpack.

Once home, I went to the freezer and grabbed my poison of choice. Ever since Ben and Jerry's retired my favorite flavor, I've been floating between new ones, looking for the one flavor to rule them all. Alas, I haven't found it yet. I settled on one with a chocolate ice cream base.

While perusing my ice cream stash, I looked to see what I would have for dinner. Knowing my limited kitchen ability, my Aunt Rose placed several frozen meals in my freezer. I chose randomly and followed the instructions she had taped to the front of the container. According to the directions, it would be at least forty-five minutes before the food was ready. That gave me plenty of time to finish off my ice cream. Luckily for me, the container was only half full.

After dinner, I was putting the dishes into the dishwasher when the wall phone rang. I still had my grandmother's landline connected. I liked the idea that if the power went out and I had forgotten to charge my phone, which happened more often than not, I'd still be able to reach the outside world.

I stood staring at it while it rang. No one called me on the landline—well, no one that I knew. The last time I answered the phone, it had been a telemarketer telling me my auto repair warranty needed to be replaced. Considering I drove a motorcycle or my grandmother's old car, I sincerely doubted the veracity of the call.

I slowly inched towards the phone as though it might bite me. I slowly lifted the receiver.

"Hello?"

"Hello, I'm looking for Ryan. This is Braden Mitchel."

I pulled the phone away from my face and looked at it, then put it back to my ear.

"Hello, are you there?" I heard him ask again. This time with less certainty.

"Oh, yes, I'm here. Hello Braden." I paused, then asked, "How did you get my number?"

"There is a very old-fashioned thing called a phone book. And your landline is listed in it."

"I forgot about that."

"How are you doing?"

"Better, it was a crazy day."

"Were you okay after I left? You seemed pretty upset."

"I have panic attacks. Sometimes I can breathe through them and let them pass, sometimes not. I was able to let this one pass today. So, it wasn't as bad as it could have been."

"I noticed that you were struggling. I wanted to get her out of there. Tammy seemed to be the cause of the attack. Does she always trigger a panic attack?"

"Sometimes she does. Sometimes it isn't as bad." I hopped up on the counter. I would do this when Annie called when we were in high school. It took me two tries. It was a lot easier when I was fourteen. "Today was a double dose."

"She went back after I left?"

"She did. She wanted to tell me that I was not woman enough for you and that she wanted me to bump her up on the wait list for a book she wanted." Why did I tell him that? I must be more exhausted than I thought.

"I think that you are more than enough for me."

I could feel my blush start somewhere around the roots of my hair and spread down to my toes.

"Um, thanks?"

"I can't believe she is still harassing you."

"You and me both. I thought that graduation and a few years of growing up would have cured her, but alas, she is uncured. I hear she is an equal-opportunity bully and harasses a lot of people."

"Wow, I knew she had it in for you in high school, but what is her problem now?"

"Not a clue. What do you mean you knew she had it in for me?"

"Back then, she saw you as a threat, I guess. When you rode up on that motorcycle that first day of class, every boy in the parking lot suddenly fell in love with you."

"I sincerely doubt that. No one ever asked me out in high school. Except for Senior Prom. Though now that you mention it, that was when she put the bullying into overdrive. I think you're exaggerating about the boys, though."

"Nope, that was a fact—as much a fact as your cousins threatening broken arms to anyone caught looking at you. Those two are very protective of you. I think that some of the guys thought that once the older one graduated, Jason wouldn't be able to hold us off. But he was very successful in his intimidation."

"I guess he was—no wonder I never got asked out. Huh," I squirmed around on the counter, trying to get comfortable. I don't remember my legs falling asleep like this. "Is that why you never talked to me?"

"Partly. I was intimidated by your cousins, just like everyone else. But also, I was shy and intimidated by you."

"I was so shy and constantly having an anxiety attack that the wind could have blown me over. Not sure how that was intimidating." Thinking back on high school, I wondered how anyone had noticed me. I tried hiding in my locker once to escape talking to someone who said good morning. A lot of people noticed that. I now realize I probably went about things the wrong way.

"Maybe, but not when you had Annie next to you or when you were on your bike. Then you seemed invincible."

"I felt invincible back then. I have more than learned my lesson. One spill during the summer between Junior and Senior year taught me a lot. It took me a little while to get back on the bike."

"How did you get the motorcycle? I always wondered. You were so shut down during our Sophomore year. I never really knew what happened."

I thought back to that year. There were more bad memories associated with my tenth-grade year than at any other time in my life up to the present. My mind went back to the day that changed so much in my life.

I had just gotten off the school bus. We lived with my grandmother then, my mother and I. She worked during the day, and my grandmother worked the night shift at the hospital. She had been a nurse since my mother was a child. I never went home to an empty house; there was always someone there.

As I walked up to the house, I found my grandmother sitting in her car. The engine was off, and her door was open. It was as though she was in the process of getting out, but gave up. I stopped next to the car and leaned in. Her face had tear stains, and she looked awful.

"Grammy, what's wrong?"

She reached out and took my hand. She didn't let go as she got out of the car. It was early in March, so the weather was cold, and I noticed she didn't have a coat on.

"Grammy, let's get in the house." I led her up the steps to the door.

She sat at the table, and I put the kettle on. I knew she liked to have a cup of tea when she felt down.

"Sweetie, sit here." She motioned to the chair next to her. "I need to tell you something," she stopped talking as the tears streamed down her face. She had barely put her head down on the table, giving into the sobs that were now wracking her body, when the door opened. My aunts Janet and Rose came through. They both looked to be in the same condition as my grandmother.

"What's going on? What happened?" I looked between the two women waiting.

"Ryan, honey," Janet sat down and took my hand. Rose stood nearby, leaning on the counter. "Your mother passed away earlier. She was in an accident. They aren't sure what exactly happened. Someone went through a light and hit her car. They must have been going pretty fast, cause they hit your mom's car really hard. They took her to the hospital." I waited, hoping that she would say that my mom was in the hospital and would be okay. "She didn't make it." She rubbed my back in small circles. "Sweetie, I am so sorry."

Janet held out her arms, and I fell into them. I couldn't cry at first. I couldn't do anything. Everything was so out of focus. My body felt far away, and the only thing I knew was the pain that was wrapping itself around me. When she placed her lips on my head in a gentle kiss, the same way my mother did, the tears started. I don't know that they have ever really stopped. The tears only fall on the inside now.

What I ended up telling Braden was, "When I was a sophomore my mother died in a car accident. I moved in with my aunt and uncle after the funeral. It was decided that I needed to be somewhere with adults in the house at night. My grandmother felt like changing now, after so many years, would be too hard on her system. In one fell swoop, I lost my mother and my home."

When I finished telling Braden, he was silent for a minute. When he did speak, I could hear the sadness in his voice. "I'm so sorry. I never knew. I knew that something had happened, but I never knew what."

"Thanks."

"How does the motorcycle play into this?"

"I wasn't coming out of the depression after my mother died. My aunt and uncle put me in therapy to help me process her death. One of the things the therapist said was that grief doesn't go away. It just changes. And that change isn't good or bad. It's just change. Anyway, I was going to therapy, and she suggested to my aunt that I get something, anything that I could put my interest into."

"That sounds like a good plan. What happened?"

"One day after school had let out for the summer, my uncle showed up with a motorcycle in the back of his pickup. It needed some work, but it looked good. My cousins were excited and hurried over to the truck to check it out. While they were talking to my uncle, my aunt pulled me aside. I had been watching from the kitchen window. Always watching, not interacting. She handed me a paper that listed a class on motorcycle safety."

Climbing off the counter, I went to sit at the table. My legs had well and truly fallen asleep, and I barely made it to the chair.

Talking about all these things brings all the familiar feelings of pain and loss. They weren't as sharp as they once were, and they didn't feel like sharp glass rubbing against me; they were just scratches against my heart. It hurt, but not as deeply, more like a dull ache that never really went away.

"I took the motorcycle class. And I helped my uncle fix the motorcycle. We took the whole thing apart and put it back together. I did all the repairs on that bike the entire time I had it. I turned sixteen at the end of July, and we went down to the DMV and got my license.

And the rest, as they say, is history. I worked part-time for my uncle to pay for the insurance, which was not cheap, and gas money."

"Wow, you really are cool."

We both laughed at that.

"What did you do after you graduated," I asked.

"I went to college near my grandparents. We lived with them for a while when I was young. My grandfather got a job offer in another part of the state and went there. My mother bought the house from them. It was an opportunity to spend time with them and have free room and board while I went to school. I tried to pay them, but they wouldn't take anything from me. I started doing all the things around the house that needed doing that my grandfather was getting too old to do. After I graduated, I got a job at a nearby high school where I had done my student teaching. I still lived with them. But when this job became available, they told me to take it and move back here. They said they didn't need a babysitter anymore. I got the job, and here I am."

I looked at the clock above the sink and sighed. It was almost midnight. I had to let him go. I needed to get some sleep, and so did he if he was going to teach a herd of teens the next day.

"I need to go." I tried unsuccessfully to stifle a yawn. "If I don't climb into bed soon and sleep, I am not going to function tomorrow. We are down one already. I don't think Annie would be particularly friendly if I were a no-show."

"You're right." I could hear his movements through the phone line. "I didn't realize how tired I was until you said something. Goodnight, Ryan."

"Goodnight, Braden."

I waited silently until I heard the line go dead. Looking around the kitchen, I determined that it was in perfectly fine shape for the night, regardless of the dishes I hadn't put away yet. Turning toward the hallway, I made my way to the bedroom and slept.

Chapter 6

Ryan

I got to the library early to start putting the display together. The encounter with Tammy threw me off enough that I left before I'd done anything about the display. I started by pulling all the books on Braden's list off the shelves. I had my music playing in my earbuds while I worked. I was getting into the song and belting out the lyrics when the cart I was pulling suddenly stopped.

A hand landed on my shoulder, causing me to both scream and jump, which caused Annie to scream in response. Between the two of us, it sounded like we were auditioning for a horror film.

"What the heck is wrong with you? You don't just grab someone." I was trying to calm my heart down while taking deep breaths. I had to lean on the cart for balance.

"Me! What the heck was that for? I have been trying to get your attention, and then you scream like you're about to be murdered." Annie leaned against the bookshelves, clutching her heart. "I came in early to help you get set up. I feel like I just ran a marathon. What is wrong with you?"

"Oh, Thanks." I straightened up when I caught my breath. "I was lost in my thoughts."

"I could tell. I forgot you had such a nice voice. You never sing anymore."

Annie took the list and looked at the stack of books I had placed on the cart. She started pulling some titles. "Where are we going to put this? Do you have any ideas?"

"I was thinking about that. We could move things around and put them in the reading room. The room that teens hang out in after school."

"We would have to rearrange the tables to get it to fit. Do you have some shelves in mind?"

"I think there is a small shelf in the storage room. We could set it up on a table so that no one had to get on the floor to see what was on the bottom shelf. What do you think? Will it be big enough?"

"That might work. If I remember right, the shelf is wide, not tall. We would need some help."

At that moment, someone started pounding on the door. We both jumped again. This time, at least, neither of us screamed. I went to the door and peeked through the curtain.

"Hello, Janet," I said as I opened the door to let her in. The lock turned a lot easier. The maintenance people must have taken care of it after we closed. It wasn't only Janet who came in, but the entire book club. "You do know that the library isn't open yet," I said as they pushed past me. "I thought the book club met at ten thirty.

"We do," She said as she moved past me. When I turned around after locking the door, I saw that the other book club ladies had set up some plates of muffins and pastries on the checkout counter. My aunt finished things out with a carafe and some cups.

"What is all this," Annie asked as she took a muffin from the tray.

"We haven't had a chance to talk in a while, so we decided to come early and see if you girls wanted some treats." The other members of the club nodded in agreement.

My Aunt Janet was the leader of this group. My other aunt was also a part of the group, but I didn't see her anywhere.

"Where's Rose?"

"Oh, she said she'd be late." At that moment, I could hear tentative knocking at the door.

Rose came in muttering her apologies for being late. "Did I miss anything?" Everyone was shushing her while she put her offerings on the counter.

"So, what you're actually here for is to grill me on yesterday's events while you bribe me into compliance with baked goods."

"That would be accurate." Janet picked up a pastry for me and put it on a napkin.

"Fine, I will tell you everything that happened yesterday if you all help us set up a display."

Everyone nodded and put their things behind the counter.

"Start talking," Rose said.

We all had some sweet tea. I had expected some form of coffee to go with the pastry, but the tea was a nice change. Then I told them about the bee.

"That's it," Janet asked. "We go to the trouble of baking your favorite treats, I even asked Connie what your favorite baked goods are, and this is all we get? A bee flew in your shirt?"

"Yes," I said. The pastries really were delicious. I felt bad for not having more exciting things to tell them. Then I also told them about Tammy coming into the library.

"We're proud of you for standing your ground. That must have been very hard." One of the club members said from behind me. Because they were all chewing, I didn't recognize the voice.

"Thanks. It was hard.I had my melt down after she left."

My aunt patted my shoulder. Everyone that I'm close to knows about my anxiety. I have been having stealth attacks for a long time. Sometimes, the anxiety is so bad that people around me can tell I'm having them. Most of the time, I have silent ones. The only way people can tell I am is when my face goes blank, and I seem not to focus on what is happening around me. Most people assume I'm daydreaming. Those who know me know differently. With Tammy being the main cause of the attacks, it never felt safe to have them "out loud" the way most people seemed to have them. Those attacks would have been blood in the water to her.

We all moved into the room where the students tended to gather after school and looked around.

"Where did you think this would work?" Janet was looking around the room, trying to see what I was describing.

"If we put the tables like this," I said as I drew it out on a piece of scrap paper. "We can create study areas, and the books can take a prominent place.

Mabel grabbed the paper and started to turn it in different directions, and then looked around the room. "I think that we should move it this way. Then it doesn't interrupt the flow of energy in the room."

Florie grabbed the paper from her. "You read way too many of those decorating books. We need to put it like this." Then she used a pencil to redraw some of the placements. "There, this will work."

She handed me back the paper. I looked at it. Then I handed it to Annie. "What do you think?"

"I think this could work very nicely," Annie replied.

Together, we moved the heavy tables into the new configurations. Some of the tables took four of us to move. When we finally got everything settled except the books, everyone looked around at our work.

"Do you think Frank will freak out when he comes back? You know he hates change," Annie said. She had a point. Frank didn't say anything about changing things up. He also hadn't said anything about the need for a display either.

"Well, he should have done something about this before he left. Like, tell us about it." Maybe I was being a little passive-aggressive, but he did more or less let this explode on us.

"If it is okay, we'll take the rest of the goodies and start the book club a little early." Janet was already gathering up the goodies when

Annie made a quick grab for the muffins. She grabbed one for me and one for herself. Annie only smiled at her when Mabel acted as though she would take them back.

I watched the group start to head off. "Thanks, Janet, Rose, Mabel, Elsie, Florie. I appreciate the help." They waved at me as they entered the room called the 'Book Cave' and closed the door.

"I guess we should open the front door." I looked at the clock as Annie moved toward the door. It had taken us an hour to get everything set up. I thought it would take all morning. And for the first time, I was glad I had some juicy tidbits to share about my life. Annie and I would never have been able to do it all alone.

We opened the door to all the people waiting outside. A steady trickle of people passed through, keeping us busy for the first hour. When things calmed down, I moved to the display and started putting the books on the shelves

I was putting the last book on the display shelf when I felt someone staring at me. It was a weird, tingly feeling between my shoulder blades. I turned to find myself under scrutiny from a very small pirate.

"Well, hello there. No dinosaur today?"

"No. We started reading Treasure Island. So, today, I am a pirate."

I noticed the small dinosaur sitting on his shoulder. "That is a very interesting parrot."

"This is a Pterodactyl. Not a parrot." He would have won first prize if awards could have been given for disdain.

"I'm sorry. My mistake."

"What are you doing?"

"We're setting up some books for the high school students to check out."

"So, will this be the high school room, like the children's room?"

"Not quite."

"Huh." With that parting remark, he turned and made his way down to the Children's room. His aunt smiled and waved, following him down the stairs.

Annie looked at me from the desk. "I love that kid. I wish I had been as sure of myself at that age."

"Think it will change when he gets to school?"

"I hope not. We need more people like him."

I moved toward the doorway and watched him meander his way to the stairs. He took a circuitous route, down one aisle and then up another. His aunt followed casually behind, periodically stopping long enough to pick out a book. She had three or four by the time she got to the stairs.

She once told me that she didn't mind the meandering path. It gave her a chance to look at the books in the stacks. She also said that sometimes books tend to leap out at her in an epic effort to be read. It was easy to see where his imagination came from.

She waved before going down the stairs. We waved back. We could hear a small voice asking her who she was waving at. When she said the librarians, we heard an "Oh." And then a little head poked around the doorway before he yelled, "Bye!" and waved.

I turned back to the display and pulled out my phone. I fired off a text to Braden and a picture of the display. I didn't expect a reply since he was at school and was surprised when his text popped up. He sent back a smiling face emoji.

I showed Annie. We both started laughing and went back to our work.

"So, you have his phone number."

"Is that a statement or a question?"

She turned around and looked at me. "I think it is a piece of information that you didn't share with the class earlier. And I am wondering why. You barely said anything about him. Even when Florie asked you."

"There are some things in my life that I would like to keep private." With that parting remark, I shut the door to Frank's office.

"You can't hide in there all day. You will have to face me. And I will require more information." Annie spoke loud enough to be heard and just shy of yelling.

By the time the book club had concluded its meeting, it was lunchtime. We took turns taking lunch breaks. Sometimes, one of us would run across the street to the pizza place and grab something for us to share if neither of us brought anything or if we planned, in advance, to grab something. Thursday was our pizza day for lunch.

On Tuesdays, I brought my lunch, and if the weather was good, I would sit out at the table under the tree and eat while watching the people go by. We had set the table up in the front lawn area of the library as a resting and gathering spot. The library wasn't very far from the park. By putting a picnic table out front, we found that people would stop and rest or gather to talk. They also came into the library

While I was sitting outside eating, I noticed the teens wandering down the sidewalk from the high school. I knew that they had had the day off the day before, so I was surprised it was an early release day. I felt old when I quietly said something along the lines of, "We never had this much time off when I went to high school."

Because of the early out, the students were showing up at the library earlier than usual. I hurried through what was left of my lunch and went inside. I wanted to see what their reactions were to the new arrangement. I also wanted to see how my book selections worked out.

Chapter 7

Braden

I loved the picture of the display Ryan sent. When I saw her text, my whole body smiled.

Sitting next to Lydia during my study hall period is usually a mistake. She grabbed the phone out of my hand and looked at Ryan's message. She wiggled her eyebrows at me.

I looked at it again. It was just a text about the display and a picture. I looked at Lydia and then down at the screen again.

"What?" I pointed at the screen.

"You know what," Lydia said, wiggling her eyebrows at me again.

"Why do you do that with your eyebrows?"

"Are you kidding me? Your entire body lit up like a strobe light." Lydia rolled her eyes and looked back down at my phone.

"It did not." I might have pouted that last statement.

"It totally did, Mr. Mitchel." One of the girls sitting at a nearby desk piped in.

"See," Lydia laughed at me as she turned around to face the girl.

"Is there no such thing as privacy?" I was beginning to feel picked on.

That comment got a laugh out of Lydia, which surprised the girl sitting at the desk in front of us. "Not in high school," Lydia said.

"That is so true," the girl said. "The other day, I was at my locker when my phone alarm went off, and my friend announced to everyone that it was time for me to take my medication."

The girl sitting next to her turned around in her chair to face us. "You know that I was telling *you*, not everyone. You forget two seconds after the alarm goes off, and you know it. Your mom told me to remind you. It wasn't my fault, I was already halfway down the hall when it went off."

"Did you have to yell it at me?"

"Would you have heard me if I whispered? No. No, you would not. And then do you know who would have been in trouble when your mom found out you didn't take your meds again? Me, that would be me."

I looked over at Lydia, who was staring at the girls. With mock judgment, I said, "Look what you started?"

She rolled her eyes at me and handed me back my phone.

The bell rang, causing me to look at the clock in confusion."Why are the classes short?"

"Early release," Lydia said.

"Why? Do we have more meetings? I thought we had them all yesterday?"

Lydia just shrugged her shoulders.

The rest of the day was filled with inservice meetings. During one of those meetings, Lydia told the other two about the message.

"Dude." With Stan, that one word could mean any number of things, from disgust to excitement. There was no way I would say anything about the implications he was making with that one word.

The messages in our group chat were flying fast and furious. I refused to tell them anything, which didn't stop the speculation. Stan almost got us caught when he forgot to turn off the keyboard sound on his phone. Lydia took it away from him and shut off the sounds before handing it back.

"How will I know if I am touching the right key," Stan asked.

"Try looking at the message before you send it," Brian said.

The principal had chosen a word to represent the theme of the meeting; the word for the meeting was Teamwork. The word for the meeting is generally chosen arbitrarily. The principal may have planned it, but it always seemed to be thrown in at the last minute. As though the whole talk was an afterthought, and the only way she could have made it make any sense was to announce a theme. We never knew beforehand what it would be. I won the word count for the times that she said "fluid." She said it twenty-five times—a world record. Teamwork only five.

By the time the meetings were over, and I was free from school, the library had already closed. Ryan had said she had a family thing and wouldn't be home, so no phone call. I hadn't realized how much I would miss talking to her. Another day, another plan to visit the library to see her.

Wednesday morning came too fast and at the same time too slowly. I watched carefully as I drove to the school for a motorcycle-riding Librarian. I hadn't seen her in over twenty-four hours, and I was feeling the loss. I hadn't felt this excited to see anyone in a long time. I think it was high school the last time I felt this, and if I remember correctly, it was Ryan then also.

My first class of the day was preparation time. Lydia was jealous of my slow start to the day. She had said repeatedly that she wished she could ease into the school day and not feel like she was waiting for a jack in the box to explode with the arrival of students to her classroom.

I used the time to text Ryan and ask her about her evening and how the afternoon had gone.

Braden*: How did the afternoon go?*

Ryan*: Wow*

Braden*: What?*

Ryan*: Punctuation. Ooh, look, I did it too! You must teach English*

Braden*: Punctuation is a valid way to convey intent and meaning in any writing form.*

Ryan: *Yup. English teacher.*

Braden: *At least I use words. Half the population communicates in emojis as though they were modern-day hieroglyphs.*

Ryan: *That would be hieroglyphs.*

Braden: *Thank you for that.*

Ryan: *To answer your question...it went well. Did you see what I did there? More punctuation.*

Braden: *Are you going to let that go?*

Ryan: *Probably not.*

Braden: *Are you at the library today?*

Ryan: *All day/*

Braden: *See you this afternoon.*

Ryan: *There is a dinosaur here. Got to go.*

I put my phone away when I heard the bell ring for classes to release. How long had I been staring at our conversation?

The students coming through the door seemed less reserved than an English class deserved. The first thing they wanted to talk about was the library. I was a little surprised. Usually, they didn't talk about anything.

Once everyone was settled, I asked if they had chosen books. Hands shot up in the air. The most vocal ones were the ones who had chosen graphic novels. Some of them were students who fought me on reading anything other than what was mandatory. I would need to apologize for doubting Ryan. The format gave them a sense of accomplishment. The ones who had read the graphic novelization of a novel talked about going to check out the novel and read it to get more details.

The readers who never read anything without the threat of failing the class seemed to be rethinking their stance on the library books.

My walk to the library after school was much more of a controlled run than a walk. As I walked through the library doors, I was hoping to see Ryan at the desk. Instead, I saw a small pirate leaning on the counter, talking to Annie. I got in line behind the pirate and blatantly eavesdropped on the young man.

"Is Ryan here," the pirate asked.

"She is, but she is busy right now." Annie leaned forward on the desk, looking the pirate in the eye.

"Oh, I wanted to show her my new dinosaur." The pirate seemed to shrink a little.

"Can you show me? I love your outfits and how much you know about dinosaurs."

"I guess so." He turned and showed Annie the small dinosaur perched on his shoulder.

"Wow, that one is cool." I looked closely at the dinosaur. It didn't seem likely that a pirate would want a miniature Tyrannosaurus on their shoulder. But times change.

"Annie," he asked in a whispered voice."Do you think Ryan would be my friend?"

"I am fairly certain that she already is," Annie whispered back. The small pirate had a huge smile as he turned and walked over to the woman waiting for him.

I stepped up to the counter. "I think I have some serious competition."

"Oh, probably," Annie raised her eyebrow at me.

"Is Ryan here?"

"Ryan is on the phone, but she should be out in a minute."

"Great!"

I went into the room where she had set up the display. There were a lot fewer books than the picture Ryan had sent, which was encouraging.

I turned and saw Ryan come out of the office. Just as I started walking toward her, one of my students asked me a question about the books. I answered them as quickly as I could and started towards the counter. When I got closer, I saw Tammy standing there with one of my students beside her. The student looked like she would rather be anywhere else.

"My sister, Dee," Tammy gestured towards the girl next to her, "can't find the book she wants on those shelves. It is on the list, but you don't have it."

"Tammy, I don't need that one book. I can read something else." I didn't think Dee's voice could have sounded more long-suffering if she tried.

"But you should be able to read the book you wanted." Tammy didn't even look at Dee when she answered. Her glare was directed at Ryan.

"If there is a book you want, I could put you on a list for it, and when it comes back, I can call you." I watched as Ryan shifted the conversation. She was talking to Dee. Her entire attention was focused on Dee.

"That would be great. I saw that there were a couple of books on the list you posted that aren't there right now. Do you have another copy of the list I can look at?" Dee's voice was much lighter than the one she used with her sister.

Ryan turned and grabbed a list off a shelf. She handed it to Dee. It was educational watching her interact with the students. I guess to her, they weren't students. They were, what did she call them, Patrons.

I moved closer so I could hear the rest of the conversation and get an idea of what books were popular with the students.

Tammy must have seen me in her peripheral vision because she turned and gave me a huge smile. Her smile was so predatory, I was ready to run out the door and hide. The same way I hid in high school whenever I saw her coming.

She had a single focus in High school: to prove that she was the *most*. It didn't matter what it was. She would be the most popular, the most beautiful, the most sought-after. Always the most. To me, she was always the most problematic.

My mother always told me that behaviors had a reason behind them. No matter how I looked, I couldn't figure out her reason. I asked my grandfather about it once. He said that some people are just insecure or feel threatened easily. He also noted that some are just mean and that it wasn't easy to tell sometimes.

As Tammy turned toward me, I knew my flight or fight expression was on my face by her slight smile.

"Well, Braden, how are you? What brings you here?" If she was trying to be sultry. She pulled it off pretty well. However, her sultriness always seemed contrived and not natural. More like a spider luring you into her web.

"Books," I said. "Why else would I come to the library? I wanted to see how the display was working out."

"I thought maybe you were here to see me," she said, leaning against the counter and tipping her head.

"How would I know you'd be here?"

She shrugged her shoulders as she stepped away from the counter, moving closer to me. She was trying to herd me away from the desk the same way I had tried to herd her out of the office that first day. I didn't move. This brought her way too close to me. If I didn't step back, she would be right up against me. I looked over to see that Dee was done talking to Ryan and had moved off. Ryan was looking at me with a wide smile. She could see my discomfort and was laughing. I knew that if Tammy turned around, that smile was going to morph into panic.

I put my hands on Tammy's shoulders and moved her to the side as I stepped around her.

"Ryan, I have a question about some other books I'd like to get on the shelf. Do you have a minute?"

"Sure," her voice was a little unsteady. Tammy was trying to elbow me out of the way.

"I'm not done with my conversation with Ryan."

"It seemed as though you were done," I said as I kept advancing toward Ryan.

Annie took that moment to step in front of Ryan. "I can help you with your problem," she said to Tammy. Effectively shoving Ryan toward the office. "Circulation is something I am very familiar with. What books are you having trouble getting?"

Ryan quickly stepped into the office. I didn't wait to be invited and moved in quickly behind her.

"Wow, she just doesn't stop, does she?" I said quietly as I looked over my shoulder, catching a glimpse of the evil stare Tammy was sending in Ryan's direction. I closed the door. Closing off Tammy's view of us.

I watched as Ryan sat down behind the desk. "Not sure what I'm going to do when Frank gets back. This has been a nice haven when she comes in. I guess I'll go back to hiding in the stacks."

I laughed at the thought of Tammy moving through the stacks in a hide-and-seek game with Ryan. Then I stopped laughing. The idea of Ryan having to hide from someone so that she could feel safe made me angry. No one should have to feel like that.

"Why do you feel you need to hide?"

"Really?" Ryan sighed and leaned back in her chair. "Weren't you there in high school? She was always like this. Sometimes, it's just easier if I hide. For whatever reason, she's always had it in for me. More so than she was with most other girls. I never figured it out then, and I still don't know. I'm not sure I want to know."

She leaned forward in her chair towards me. "What did you want to talk to me about? Did we do okay with the books we added to the list?"

"The books are great. The students I talked to today were thrilled with the list. They seemed to like your choices more than mine."

"Is this the first time you put one of these lists together," Ryan asked.

"Is it obvious? Where I taught before, they were pretty strict about the books you could teach or assign as reading. That's why I thought I would take it outside the classroom. Thank you for doing this."

"You're welcome. Was there something else?"

"I wanted to ask you to go out for dinner tonight."

Her brow came down as she thought about what I asked. "You want to go on a date?"

"Yes?" It came out as a question. I was beginning to wonder if I had said something wrong. I thought back over what I had said. Nope, that was pretty straightforward.

"Tonight?"

"Yes." This time, I had a definitive answer.

"Okay?" Now her answer sounded like a question.

"Do you like pizza," I asked.

"Yes, I love pizza."

"Great. We can go across the street when you get done."

We both got up to leave the office. When we got to the counter, she turned with a somewhat panicked expression.

"Oh, no. I rode my motorcycle today. I don't like riding it home in the dark."

Annie jumped up to the counter. "I can pick you up for work in the morning. I'm sure Braden won't mind driving you home." She looked over at me for confirmation. I nodded, wondering how she knew what we were talking about.

"It would be my honor to drive you home." I was thrilled to have the opportunity to spend more time with her. Ryan looked a little leery at first.

"Okay, that'd be great."

"Good. I'll meet you out front when you close up here." I left as quickly as I could so that she didn't have time to change her mind. I knew she struggled with anxiety. And I didn't want her to work herself up to say no because she felt panicked.

I ran back to the school and got my car from the faculty parking lot. I parked in front of the restaurant and then settled myself at the table in front of the library and pulled out my book.

Chapter 8

Ryan

I watched Braden make his quick exit.

"He probably raced out, so you couldn't change your mind." Annie elbowed me.

I was in shock. Someone asked me out. He obviously had not heard of my previous dating disasters. Probably because he just moved back and managed to miss that gossip. In reality, there hadn't been that many. Only a few very well-talked-about instances—one involving the fire department.

"I guess he missed the memo on dating me."

"Or he just doesn't care."

Annie pushed me out the door a few minutes early. I was surprised to see Braden sitting at the picnic table. He had been watching for me and jumped up, gathering his things together as soon as he saw me. His car was parked in front of the restaurant, enabling him to put his stuff in as we passed it.

As he reached to open the restaurant's door, I grabbed him and pulled him to the side of the doorway.

"I'm not good at this?"

"What, eating?"

"No, dating. I have many horror stories—well, not many, but more than anyone should have. And I am scared that you will be like the others and not want to talk to me afterward."

"I sincerely doubt that will happen." He paused and looked away, obviously thinking. Was he trying to think of a way out of this? "To take the pressure off," he began, "Why don't we act like we did the other night when we talked on the phone? There was no pressure. Just friends getting to know each other again. The only difference is that we can see each other." He waited patiently for me to say something.

"I can do that."

"Good. Ready?"

This time, I let him open the door. As we went in, I looked around for a table. I saw one in the back, out of direct view of the rest of the restaurant.

"Is that okay?" I pointed, and he nodded. As I led the way to the table, the waitress saw us and nodded at me.

When she got to the table to give us menus and take a drink order, she picked up the candle and blew it out before removing it. Was it embarrassing? Yes. Was it usual? For me, yes.

"Why did you do that?" Braden asked, taking the candle back from her and putting it on the table.

"It's the policy."

"Really? Because other tables have candles."

"It's okay," I said.

"No, it isn't. Just leave the candle even if it isn't lit." The waitress looked confused as to what to do. She had always removed the candle.

"Okay." She still seemed unsure about what to do with the candle. She rallied and fell back on routine. "Do you know what you want to drink?" We placed our orders.

After she left, I tried to think of an explanation that would be the least embarrassing.

"The story with the candle," I paused, looking around the restaurant to see if anyone was looking. "Well, it's kind of an embarrassing story. One of those dating nightmares I mentioned."

He just smiled at me, waiting.

"So," I paused. Desperately trying to think of a way to make this less embarrassing for me. "I was on a date. He had ordered a beer. I don't drink, by the way. Anyway, I knocked the table with my leg, which I was bouncing because I was nervous, and bounced his beer when he went to set it down. It spilled on the table and then on him. Then, when I went to clean it up with my napkin, I knocked the candle over." I looked at Braden, and I could see he was trying hard not to laugh. "Then the candle kind of caught the napkin on fire. I dropped the burning napkin into the beer, which flamed for a minute. Honestly, I didn't think it would do that. I didn't think there was enough alcohol in it for it to combust like that. And then, one of the patrons called the fire department. But by the time they got here, it was all put out. No fire."

Braden was laughing. He couldn't stop laughing.

"After that, the policy is that they put out the candle when I am sitting at a table. It's a bit overkill, actually, but that's why she tried to take the candle."

"Are you nervous now?"

"No, well, a little. But not like I was that night."

When the waitress came back, Braden asked her to relight the candle. When she paused, he told her that it would be fine, that nothing was going to happen. Surprisingly, because they never did it when I asked, she lit the candle.

"A whole new start. New memories," he said.

I smiled at him, and for the first time, I didn't feel nervous about being on a date.

We spent the rest of the evening talking, much like we did on the phone. We stayed with topics that were comfortable. I was very aware of Braden watching me. Even though his conversation was natural and fun, he saw when the level of my anxiety changed. It could have been caused by a topic or someone too close to me, and he'd distract me with a funny story from his earlier teaching job.

I turned when someone sat at the next table. A man I had dated once sat down. He looked over at us and gave a weird shoulder shrug to

Braden. I felt like a deer in the headlights. Shame from the way the date had gone, anxiety at being out in the world, and fear of messing this up with Braden all fought for supremacy in my brain.

Braden reached over and put his hand on mine. "I meant to ask about your pirate admirer."

"My pirate admirer?"

"He was in front of me in line at the library earlier. A little guy with a dinosaur on his shoulder."

"Oh, him. He is adorable. Sometimes, he comes in as a dinosaur. His Aunt is reading Treasure Island. He's shown up as a pirate the last few days. He is very into dinosaurs. Which is why he has one instead of the usual parrot."

"He asked Annie if she thought you would be his friend."

I sat back, placing my hand on my heart. A slow smile spread over my face. "That boy is going to break my heart."

"So, this is my competition? A pirate with a dinosaur on his shoulder?"

"Well, he has been winning my heart for a long time."

Braden laughed. "I see. Well, the competition may be tough, but I think I can put up a good fight."

When we finished the meal and left the restaurant, I was feeling relaxed and happy.

"I meant to ask you if you needed anything else," he motioned to what I was carrying. "I mean your motorcycle equipment."

"No, I'll ride it home after work tomorrow. I left the jacket and helmet in the library so I won't have to lug them back in the morning."

"Right, I forgot about that."

He opened the car door for me. I don't remember anyone ever opening the car door for me. I must have had a surprised look on my face.

"Old car," —he held up his keys and then pointed at the door. "I need to unlock it with the key."

"That's fine. I couldn't remember anyone ever opening my door for me before." I climbed into the car.

As he closed the door, I heard him mutter, "That's because they were losers."

I gave him directions to my house. We were both quiet as he drove. As he pulled into the driveway, I did what I usually do when someone else is driving. I looked at the house as though I saw it for the first time.

"How long have you lived here?" Braden's voice broke into my reverie.

"I've lived here since I got back from college."

"Only four years?" Braden looked confused.

"Well, no, I lived here before with my grandmother and mom. I was here until my mom died. Then, I lived with my aunt and uncle. I've lived here by myself for about four years."

"Was this your mom's house?"

"No, this was my grandmother's house. My mom came here after I was born."

"I remember you telling me about that."

"I moved in with my Aunt and Uncle in the Spring. The same year I got the motorcycle."

"I remember. You made quite the impression when you showed up at school that first day."

"Did I? I guess I did. I was asked a lot of questions about the motorcycle. Mostly from guys but some from the girls. It was pretty much the only time guys wanted to talk to me."

"It was probably the only conversation your cousins let them have."

"Oh."

"Your cousins are very protective. I guess they were even more protective of you after your mom died. They very effectively blocked any of the guys from asking you out. As I told you the other night on the phone."

"Right. Well, things make more sense now. I remember Annie's reaction when I showed up on the motorcycle. She watched me ride into the parking lot and was smiling when I got to her in the doorway. She would only say that things were going to get exciting soon."

"I had been waiting outside to talk to someone and saw you ride up. Everyone saw you ride up. After you walked into the building, your cousins were fighting off guys wanting to talk to you. Your cool factor went way up that day."

"I still can't believe my cousins kept everyone from asking me out in high school.

"Your cousins are great at defense and blocking. No one got past them. Believe me, I know."

"Seriously, I thought I was unattractive in high school. No one wanted to spend time with me because of my cousins?"

"Um, yes?"

"They are going to die."

I got out of the car before he could get around to opening the door. By the time he made it around the car, I was already out and closing the door.

"Thanks for having dinner with me." He put his hand in mine and walked me to the door.

"Thank you for asking me."

Unsure how this was going to go, I headed for the door. The last time someone had walked me to my door after a date, he had tried to kiss me and insinuate that he should come in. That evening did not end how he wanted it to.

I have been kissed before. Though that is a story for another day. The closer the doorstep, the more nervous I felt. Did I want him to kiss me? Yes, I did want to be kissed by him. At the same time, memories of the last time I had been kissed were invading my brain, making me more nervous.

I had my keys in my hand. I needed my other hand back so that I could open the door. I turned to Braden to say good night, and he leaned in, lightly kissing my cheek. Squeezing my hand, he said, "Good night," then walked back to his car.

"Good night." I was frozen there at my door, staring at Braden.

"I am not driving off till you go in the door and lock it behind you." I could hear laughter in his voice. That spurred me on. Now that I was utterly embarrassed by my inaction, I sped up. I waved to him as I closed the door. I turned the lock and leaned against it. That was probably the best date ever.

Chapter 9

Ryan

Annie picked me up in the morning and managed to get all the details of my date from me over cocoa and muffins at the Coffee Shop. Connie had even found a few minutes to sit with us and grill me for information. When I told Annie about my past date, who sat next to us in the restaurant, she started to seethe.

"I remember that creep. Wasn't he the one who ended the date early and then tried to get you to let him into your house?"

"What guy tried to get into Ryan's house?" Jared sat down at our table. His business partner, Owen, was with him.

"Hello, Connie," Owen said as he put his coffee on the table and leaned against the wall. Jason took the last chair.

"Hi, Owen. You can have my chair. I need to get back to work." Connie got up and left before anyone could respond.

"Why does she always leave when you arrive? You two have a history I don't know about," Jared asked.

"You could say that."

"Back to someone trying to get into Ryan's house." Jason was not going to give up on that. The Big Brother protection mode had been engaged.

"It was a long time ago. Remember that guy I went on the date with, and he tried," I let the sentence hang there. A look of remembered anger crossed his face.

"Is he still bothering you?" Jared moved his chair toward Annie to give Owen a little more room. Those two took up some serious space with their shoulders.

"What guy," Owen asked.

Jared turned toward Owen as he answered. "There was this guy who took Ryan out on a date. Ryan didn't feel safe, and when she doesn't feel safe, she gets awkward. Anyway, he had had enough of the awkwardness and ended the date mid-meal. He took her back to the house. Then tried to force his way in. Luckily, Jason had seen them leave and followed them home. Needless to say, the guy did not leave gracefully." He turned back to me, "Is he bothering you again?"

"No, nothing like that. He sat down at a table next to me when I was out with Braden, and he gave a smug look at Braden. I felt uncomfortable. That's all."

"Wait, you were out on a date last night?"

Annie tapped Jared on the shoulder. "Text me later, and I'll fill you in."

"Okay." Then back to me. "What did Braden do?"

I sighed and tried to put my head down on the table. "Braden just held my hand and asked me a question. He also glared at the guy. He made me forget the other guy was there by talking to me."

"What?" Three voices said almost simultaneously.

Annie pulled me up off the table. "I can't hear you when you talk into furniture. What did you say?"

"I said, Braden kept talking to me and made me feel comfortable and distracted from the jerk next to us. He knocked the jerk's jacket on the floor from the back of his chair and walked on it as we went past."

"I liked him before, now I really like him." Annie leaned back in her chair, smiling.

"Annie, seriously?"

"What? That guy is a tool. He deserved to have his coat walked on."

Jared and Owen both stood up and pushed their chairs under the table. "We'd better head out. The shop won't open itself."

Jared leaned down and kissed the top of my head. "Stay safe. Don't let anyone give you crap. You know who I mean."

I did know who he meant. The same person he had been telling me not to take any crap from since high school.

"I will try to stay out of trouble."

"Bye, Connie." Owen walked close to the counter on his way out. The only response Connie gave was a wave as she headed into the back.

"Something is going on with those two?" Annie watched Owen's face fall a little while he watched Connie leave. "Yup, definitely something going on."

"Speaking of things opening, we need to get to the library before they storm the doors."

"No one has ever stormed the library." Regardless of any possible storming, we gathered our things and walked to the library to start our day.

I didn't hear or see Braden all day, other than a short text saying he would call that night. Tammy, however, made an appearance around lunchtime.

She was moving around the shelves. Looking at books. Reading the flaps and then putting them back. She had a list with her that she periodically checked. It was normal library behavior. It wasn't unusual for people to have lists. She would periodically look at the desk and then go back to what she was doing. I knew I was in trouble when Annie left to help someone, and Tammy made a move on the desk.

"I can't seem to find this book. The system says that it should be here." She handed me her list and pointed to one in particular. With a sigh, I came around the counter and headed into the stacks.

I was looking in all the places it could be. Then I looked in all the places someone might have accidentally reshelved it. There had been some very creative shelving through the years. The time we found

Douglas Adams in the travel section was still a favorite story in the library. Tammy followed along right behind me while I looked.

She would make exasperated sounds when I looked somewhere she had already looked. I can't even begin to count all the times someone has missed a book because it was three books over from where it should be. I couldn't even say how many times I had missed a book because it was with the next author alphabetically on the shelf.

Finally, what I had been waiting for happened.

"I heard you were out with Braden last night. Was it as bad as the other dates you went on?"

I didn't reply. I just kept looking for the book.

"Did you light the table on fire this time? Or maybe knock the food off the table by pulling the tablecloth?"

I still didn't reply. Though that last one was an accident. I thought the tablecloth was my napkin and had pulled it rather quickly in an attempt to wipe something off my chin. Also, an embarrassing moment all on its own.

After ten minutes of looking, I gave up.

"Tammy, I don't think the book is here. Why don't I put a hold on it and we try to find out where it got to."

We got to the desk, and I started to look up the book in the system. Tammy put all her books on the counter and started to look through them.

"Oh, I guess I overlooked this." She held up the book I had just spent ten minutes looking for. "My mistake. I must have already picked it up."

Granted, that had happened before. On accident. Hers was not an accident. One more way to annoy me.

"It could happen to anyone. Glad you found it." If I didn't show any emotion about it, I hoped to lessen the encounter. No food for her bullying if I didn't rise to her bait. It was wishful thinking, though.

"You think you are so much better than the rest of us. You aren't, though. You are just a little librarian. In a little library."

Why she thought that was an insult, I had no idea. "Thank you. I like being a librarian. And this is a nice little library." I handed her her freshly checked-out books. "Have a great day."

"You know you aren't fooling anyone."

"Who am I trying to fool? I work at a library and lead a very quiet life. It isn't like I'm trying to win prom queen votes through intimidation." That last one might have been a holdover from high school. Everything with this woman seemed like a holdover from high school.

"Just because you were a nobody in high school doesn't mean you can take it out on those of us who were someone."

I could feel the tingles start in my fingers. But I could also feel anger start to bubble up in my chest. "I hope you have a nice day."

I turned away from the counter and went into the office. I knew she could follow me there, and if she were in the mood to continue the conversation, she would. I was betting on her having gotten what she came for with the book harassment. I leaned against the door and waited.

There was a knock a few minutes later. A knock meant Annie. Tammy never knocked.

"Are you okay in there?"

I moved away from the door so I could open it. "I'm okay."

"She's gone. Left with her head held high and her usual look of superiority. What happened?"

I told Annie about the morning book hunt.

"I'm proud of you. I think,"

We were interrupted by a voice from the desk. "Ryan! Are you okay?"

I went out to the desk and looked over the top. There was my little pirate. His aunt was standing right behind him.

"Are you okay? I saw that lady be mean to you. You looked upset."

"I'm okay. Thank you for checking on me. You're a good friend."

He turned to his aunt, "She called me her friend!"

"Yes, she did. And you are a good friend." She placed her hand on his head and stroked down his hair. He nimbly dodged her touch. She looked up at me and smiled. "I stop in here all the time with this little guy, but I don't think I ever introduced myself. I'm Esther."She reached across the top of the pirate's head to shake hands. "This is Nate."

I reached out to shake her hand and then Nate's, since he had his hand out as well.

"It is really good to meet you." It felt really good to make new friends. "This is Annie."

"Oh, Annie and I have met before." She smiled at Annie. "How is yoga going these days?"

"I have no idea. I left shortly after you did. I had too much going on."

I was trying to think of when Annie went to yoga. She had tried to get me to go with her. I did once. I felt overwhelmed by the number of people there. It must have been shortly before Annie quit. She never asked or talked about it after that.

"We should get down to the children's area. There is a puppet show today. I'm glad you're doing okay. Bullies can be rough." She patted my hand before taking Nate's hand and heading toward the stairway.

"She's nice. I love that kid." I turned to look at Annie when she didn't respond. "You okay?"

"Yes, just thinking."

At that moment, a herd of people made their way to the counter. Maybe not a herd, but it felt like it. I let Annie take the questions while I checked out books. The afternoon moved fairly quickly after that.

When we closed up the library, I realized that I hadn't heard from Braden other than the one message.

The phone was ringing as I walked through the door. I dropped everything onto the table and reached for the phone.

"Hello."

"Hello, Ryan. Sorry, I didn't get in touch with you earlier. Seems like a jerk move to take someone out and then not call them."

"Oh, I don't know. It is a new era. I could have called you."

"True. Well then, why didn't you call me?"

"Maybe because you teach school, and I could have been interrupting your class. I don't call people very often. I do text, though. I guess that's the new way to communicate. Although this is nice. Hearing your voice."

"Wow, I think I just melted a little. I wanted to let you know before this conversation goes any further," he continued.

All I heard was before this goes any further. Thoughts of him saying it was fun but...things I had heard often in the past. All the reasons why I was just not enough.

"Ryan, are you there?"

"Yes, I'm here."

"Did you hear me? I had to go out of town this morning. My grandfather had a heart attack and we, my mother and I, are going to them. My grandmother needs some help and someone to be with her. I won't be able to see you till I get back."

"Oh, Braden, I am so sorry. Is there anything I can do to help? Do you or your mom have any animals that need caring for while you're gone?"

"No pets." There was a pause. "Thanks. You're always trying to help people."He paused before he said, "Who helps you?"

"So many people." I laughed. I thought about the morning in the Coffee Shop. How my cousin instantly started to go into protection mode. Nate and Esther reaching out to me. Annie always having my back. "So many people," I repeated.

"I'm glad. About this weekend. If I text you a lot, will I be disturbing anything?"

"Not really. I think it's game night at my Aunt's house, and the book club will be there. So, not sure how many games will get played. But I'll tell you all the gossip."

"Deal. I have to go. My Mother is signaling me. I'll text later."

"Okay. Bye, Braden."

"Bye, Ryan."

Chapter 10

Ryan

Usually, I have every other Friday off. It makes up for working every other Saturday. Frank, being on vacation, has thrown off the scheduling. I had to go to the library and work even though it was my usual Friday. I made a compromise with Annie. She would only have to work short-staffed in the morning on Friday, then I would come in during the afternoon and finish the day. I would work on Saturday as usual.

I checked the weather and then got ready to go into town. I would ride my motorcycle into town, then head to the park and spend time at my favorite quiet spot, the gazebo. The Gazebo sits closer to the street than the center of the park, and if I sit in the right place, I can watch all the comings and goings around town. The position from the gazebo meant I could see down Main Street.

This serves two purposes: I can people-watch, and I can watch for Tammy. She had upped her bullying after my date. The day of the book incident, she came back later and did her routine of dropping little demeaning remarks. Nothing you could call her on. Subtle comments meant to chip away at self-worth and create uncertainty. Due to all her years of practice, she was a professional at the subtle jab.

The ride to the library was wonderful. The leaves were an amazing, vibrant green. Riding in the fall with the leaves changing colors was beautiful. But to me, the spring brought a beauty that transcended the fall. The waking-up time. I felt like I was waking up as well.

The weather was warmer, and the light was stronger. Both of which made me feel more alive. I began to wonder if I could get Braden to go for a ride with me. I had an extra helmet. Though I wasn't sure if he could wear it. I'd bought it for Annie. I'd ask my cousins if they had an extra helmet. They had both gotten motorcycles after high school.

I parked at the library and placed my helmet just inside the employee door in the back. I checked my phone when it vibrated. It was another text from Braden telling me about how things were going and checking in. He and his mother had been pretty busy the night before at the hospital and seemed to still be busy. I typed a quick reply and put my phone away.

I noticed the interim pastor getting out of her car. The library shared a parking lot with the church.

My time at church had slowed to non-existent after my mother died. Once she was gone, I stopped going. Whether it was from anger at God for taking her from me, or because I couldn't face all the people at the church trying to console what couldn't be consoled, I don't know. The pastor at the time was an older man who was very rigid. He was a good man. But gentle compassion was not his thing.

Probably why my aunts and the other women became such a force within the congregation. They knew what was going on long before the pastor or anyone else. They knew if you needed help or just a hug. And they followed through with their help. I hand-delivered more casseroles and took part in more wood projects to get firewood for people than any other kid my age. My cousins were usually exempt from the casserole delivery.

I waved at the Pastor. She was something of an oddity. The only woman pastor in town. I had seen her in passing, but had never spoken to her.

"Good morning," she said as I started to walk by on my way to the park.

"Good morning."

"I'm Kate. I don't think we've met."

"Ryan Matthewson. I work at the library."

"Do you have a minute to talk? I have a few questions."

"Okay?" Unsure as to what questions I might be able to answer for her, I followed. She signaled toward the church door. We went through to her office. Kate's office was comfortable. Though a little bare. She noticed me looking around.

"It isn't easy being an interim. You don't know how much of yourself to put into the decorations since you don't know how long you'll be somewhere."

"Have you always been an interim?"

"No, not always. I spent the first few years of my ministry at the same church. I was a junior minister at that time. Working with the established minister. Then I started to accept different assignments. Hoping to find my place somewhere."

"How long are you here for?"

"That is the question. The pastor I am substituting for hasn't decided if he's going to retire or just convalesce."

"That could be problematic." I sat down in the chair facing her desk. "What can I help you with?"

"I have an older member of the congregation who needs some community. Do you know of any group that they could join in any way? Something for them to look forward to and get them out of the house."

"How old are they?"

"They're close to seventy. She lost her husband a few years back and recently moved here to live with her children."

"Does she read? Bake? Is she nosy, and does she like to butt into people's lives in a good way?"

Kate laughed. "That is oddly specific. But I think she fits into most of those. Or would if she had anyone to interact with."

"You should mention her to my aunt Janet. If you hadn't noticed, my aunt has her finger on the pulse of this town like no one else. If she doesn't know of a group, she'll put one together out of other people she has been keeping her eye on."

"I heard that I should get to know her better. I have only been here a few weeks. The woman's daughter is the one who mentioned the problem to me. They're new to the area as well. And the daughter works, so there is no one at the house during the day with her mother. And since she is new, she doesn't have any friends yet."

"Janet is your person. There is a book club that meets weekly at the library. Though weekly is a loose term for them. And I am not exactly sure that they read any books at all. But they do meet often and talk about everything and everyone. I'll mention it to my aunt when I see her this afternoon. I think the group is meeting today. Even though they just met. I think someone's nephew is having trouble with something, and an emergency meeting has been called." I held up my phone. "I get the texts. Let me say something to them now."

I typed everything that Kate had told me into my phone and sent the message. It only took a minute for my phone to start vibrating repeatedly as all the members started to answer.

"They want to know her name and contact info. Someone will be calling or knowing the book group, dropping by, and kidnapping her to a meeting."

Kate smiled and dug out the paper she'd written the contact information on. After relaying the information to me and me relaying it to the group, she looked a little concerned.

"I wasn't expecting such a quick solution."

"My aunts are very good at solutions. And they are very good at making people feel comfortable in uncomfortable situations. This woman will be right at home with them. Or if they're not a good fit. They know who would be."

"I guess I should spend some time getting to know them." She paused and looked at me for a minute before taking a breath and saying, "Do you know of any good books to read?"

I laughed this time. "What genre are you looking for?"

"Something or anything to keep me company until *I* find a group or community."

I looked at my watch. It was still early, a few hours before the library opened. "Are you busy right now? I think I know a place that could help."

As we started down the street to the Coffee Shop, I looked longingly towards the park. I could see the gazebo and my quiet morning slipping away. I smiled at Kate as we walked, listening to her talk about the other places she had been, and my longing slid away. This would be a better morning than the one I had planned.

The Coffee Shop was doing a rousing business. Mostly to go, thank goodness. I saw Annie sitting at our table. Funny how if you go somewhere often enough, you find that you have "a table."

"Hey, stranger! I wasn't expecting to see you today. I thought you were going to have a quiet morning somewhere."

"Change of plans. Annie, have you met Kate?"

"Yes, unlike some people, I go to church." She reached out and shook hands with Kate. "Hello, Pastor."

"Just Kate. Please."

"Okay, Kate." Annie gave Kate one of her welcoming smiles. Annie's smiles always make people feel welcomed and accepted. It's one of her many attributes.

"I found Kate lost and alone in the parking lot, bereft of friend and kin. So I brought her here." I waved at Connie and motioned between Kate and me. She waved back and nodded. Cocoa was incoming.

"I was not wandering around the parking lot," Kate insisted.

"What have you been reading lately? You are talking weird." Annie moved her things off the table, giving Kate and me plenty of room.

Connie showed up as we were getting situated. She put the cocoa on the table and grabbed a chair.

"Hi, I'm Connie. I've seen you here before, but we haven't said hello."

"Kate." Again, Kate put out her hand to shake.

"So, what are we talking about?" Connie settled in for a chat. I looked over and noticed that somehow she had cleared out the waiting customers. It was suddenly peaceful.

"We just sat down, literally, just sat down when you came over. We have barely finished with the hellos and introductions." Annie turned to Kate, "So, what have you been up to?"

"Well," Kate launched into a quick sum up of her life so far and how she had managed to show up in our town.

"She was free, and I invited her to come hang out and have a cup with us." I nudged Annie under the table. "She asked about someone at church who needed a friend group or community. I sent the info on to the book club. I thought that between the four of us, we should be able to come up with some ideas as well."

Chapter 11

Ryan

Monday morning was beautiful, and the weather forecast for the day was for more wonderful Spring weather. I decided to ride my bike to work again. Hopefully, avoiding any more Monday morning bees.

Frank was due back from his vacation. Which meant I didn't need to show up early. I thought I would let him get acclimated to the changes that we made while he was gone.

Frank had been at the library when I was in elementary school. He'd become the head librarian while I was in college. And he didn't like change. He did accept change when he had to, but he complained about it the whole time. If I didn't show up early, I could escape a lot of his complaining.

I decided to park at the library and go to the coffee shop for a few hours before work. Annie would show up there for the same reason. The only person who could reasonably handle Frank in a tantrum was Mabel. She had been the children's librarian for as long as I could remember. My mother would take me to her story hour when I was in preschool. Mabel was young then, just out of college. On the occasions she runs roughshod over the Book club, there is more laughing than arguing.

Walking past the bookstore, I stopped to check out the displayed titles. When I was younger, I thought about becoming a writer. That dream didn't last long. I decided I liked reading more than writing. But sometimes, I still think about what my book would look like in the display window. I leaned in to look at the cover of a new romance when I noticed movement behind me.

Looking in the window, I saw Tammy's reflection. She was crossing the road and headed for me. I didn't think; I just moved. I pulled open the door of the bookshop and walked in.

As I passed Llyod, the owner, I signaled toward the back of the shop. He looked past me toward the door and must have seen Tammy. He nodded and then moved to intercept. I had been in the store once when Tammy started following me around. The same way she did in the library. Her tactic for bullying was like water torture. She was relentless. Needless to say, Lloyd wasn't one of her biggest fans.

I went through the stock room and out the back door. An alley runs the length of the businesses on this side of the street. All the back doors open onto it. Deliveries were a lot easier when they came through the back door.

I moved quickly down the alley, counting the doors. It isn't as easy to tell which business was which without the front windows. When I reached the coffee shop, I opened the door and went inside.

The kitchen was warm and smelled like yeast and sugar—two of my favorite things. I asked Becky, Connie's assistant, if she would get Connie from the front. I found where the wonderful smell was coming from and was just leaning into the cinnamon rolls to breathe it in when Connie came in.

"I left Becky up front. What's going on? Are you okay?"

"Tammy. She was crossing the street and heading for me. I ducked into the bookstore and escaped out into the alley. Can I hide in here?" I was a little out of breath from the Tammy-induced run.

Connie looked around the kitchen. "Sure, you can use the break table. I'll bring you your usual. It's about time for my break. I'll come join you if that's okay."

"That sounds nice. Can they spare you up front?"

"Sure, Becky can handle the front for a little bit. It isn't that busy at the moment. She'll come get me if she needs help. I'll let her know you're back here so she doesn't say anything if Tammy comes in."

"You are a lifesaver." I made my way to the table while Connie went out front.

I looked into the small office tucked into the back corner of the kitchen. Connie had a desk and chair in the small room as well as an old file cabinet. She said that she rarely used the room. It was too claustrophobic. Usually, she would work at the break table or one of the small tables in the back of the dining area. Her Aunt was the same way when she ran the Coffee Shop. Connie's aunt was the reason the book club existed. They met in the dining area after the Coffee shop closed. When her aunt and grandmother decided to tour the country in a camper, the book club was already established at the library.

Connie had been a manager for a coffee shop in the city. She had grown up in the city. She spent most of her summers at her grandmother's house. Her grandmother was her aunt's business partner. Which meant that Connie was already familiar with the coffee shop and how it was run. When the two of them called her to come run things, Connie came willingly. There had been some problems with a few of the employees where she was working, and she needed a change.

Little changed in the shop when Connie took over, except for the hours. The shop was now open later in the afternoon, taking advantage of the after-school crowd and those looking for something to get them home. Other than the library, it was where you could find students in the afternoon.

I was standing, looking at pictures of the shop when it first opened, and other family pictures on the wall of the little office, when Connie walked in. She was carrying two cups. She placed the hot chocolate in front of the extra chair and her coffee in front of her spot. "I'll be right back."

When she returned, she had two plates of cinnamon rolls.

"I tried something new this morning. I used some canned pumpkin and added it to the dough. Then I used more ginger than cinnamon, and put sliced apples instead of raisins. What do you think?"

I carefully tore off a piece of the roll. When I put it in my mouth, it melted on my tongue. Closing my eyes, I let the taste flow around in my mouth.

"I'll take that expression as an answer," she said.

"This is so good."

"Thanks. I saw Tammy outside the shop. She was looking in the window, and I assume she was looking for you. Why is she following you?"

"Who knows," I told Connie about the previous week. "Luckily, I had Sunday off since the library is closed. I have no idea why she goes after me like this. It is almost pathological. I have no idea if she does it to anyone else."

"The little hidden criticisms in her statements that she repeats incessantly when she's trying to wear you down? Oh. She does it to other people. Though not as much as she does you. What's her story?"

"I wish I could tell you. She started on me when we were in elementary school. And it only got worse in high school. In high school, she wasn't so subtle about it. Even now, you would be hard-pressed to say she was doing something. All she does is ask questions or make comments. Nothing more or less than anything others have asked about, like the bee incident. Everyone else asked about it. But when they asked, it was with humor and playfulness about my disrobing in public, which is what one older woman called it. When she says it, there is a hidden nastiness to it. In high school, she had a clique to back her up and was pretty much the moving force of the school within the social groups. Her bullying got worse after my mother died."

"I never see her with anyone when she is out and about. Does she have any friends," Connie asked.

"Her friends all moved away for college and never came back. Some got married, and some had jobs in other places. Tammy just stayed. Let's talk about something else. Something less likely to bring up traumatic memories."

There was a crash as the kitchen door flew open. Connie jumped up to see what was going on.

I saw Annie through the doorway. "Hey Connie, do you have any more cinnamon rolls? And have you seen Ryan?" Annie winked at me as she held the door open, only far enough for her to look in. "Quit pushing me, Tammy. Only staff are allowed back here. Health code violations and all that."

Connie pushed Annie out of the way with the tray of cinnamon rolls. I moved so that I was not visible from the doorway. At the last second, I picked up my cup and plate. I had just moved out of sight when I heard Tammy,

"Oh, I didn't realize you were having your break back here. Seems rather lonely to sit by yourself."

"It's more peaceful than sitting with some people," Connie said as the door closed.

"I went back to the table and sat down. I wasn't sure if Connie would be back. It would be nice to talk more. But she did have a business to run.

I settled into Connie's chair. If she wasn't going to sit in it, then I may as well get comfy. She kept a special chair at the table. It seemed more suited to an office than a kitchen table. Her chair is so comfy. It even tips back. I need to find out where she got it. I could use a chair like this at my desk at home. If I tried to get this chair for the library, Annie would steal it in a heartbeat. With my e-reader in one hand and my cocoa in the other, I started reading.

I was getting into the story when the door opened, and someone came in through the back. I watched as Annie quietly came in the door. She turned, leaning against the door, looking at me.

"I have nothing to feel guilty for, so quit looking at me like that," I said as I sipped from my cup.

"Sure you don't." She came into the room and squatted down, looking at the chair. "We need these in the library."

"One, we don't sit down long enough to enjoy these chairs. And two, Frank would never order them for us. I was thinking of getting one for my office at home."

"Honestly, how much work would you get done if you could tip your chair back like that? None. That's how much work would get done."

"What are you doing back here?" I tore off a piece of the cinnamon roll and gave it to Annie.

"I came back here because Tammy is sitting out front watching for you. Since you usually come here in the mornings. I assume she is simply waiting for you to show up." She rolled her eyes heavenward while she chewed. "These are the best."

We both turned as the back door opened again. My aunts came through the door bearing takeaway cups of coffee and bags of pastries. They grabbed some of the folding chairs Connie keeps in the back for when she needed more chairs out front.

"Morning, girls," Janet said. She placed her things on the table.

"We saw the stakeout out front, and Connie told us where you were. So here we are." Rose looked around the kitchen. "I am not sure having a meeting back here is in step with the health code, but oh well." She sat down next to Janet and started handing out pastries. Rose got plates down from the shelf over the sink.

"So, why is Tammy out in the other room," Janet asked.

"I wish I knew. She started a campaign of harassment last week."

"She started really harassing Ryan after her date with the new teacher." Annie was easily bribed with food. A muffin, and she would tell all my secrets. She rarely gave away her own, but for a pastry, she would tell everything to my aunts. This was a well-known fact, which is why my aunt knew everything I did when I lived with them.

"Would it kill you for once not to blurt my secrets to the world?"

"Probably," she said around a mouthful.

"Don't talk with your mouth full. I thought you had better manners." Janet tapped Annie's arm and then reached for another muffin.

I noticed that the three of them were staring at me, waiting. I picked up my muffin and took a bite.

"So, from what I can tell, Ryan went out with Braden." Annie began telling them everything between muffin bites. "Tammy is jealous for some reason. Or, actually, who knows why she upped her harassment? She comes in and follows Ryan while she tries to find a lost book,"—the lost was done with air quotes— "and says all manner of passive-aggressive comments while following Ryan. It burns me up. But she isn't doing anything that you can call her on. Just like always."

"I remember her mother was like that in high school. She was always sly. Subtle. But very sly. Some girls were worn down by it and avoided her as much as possible. I remember one girl even changed schools to get away from her. There was nothing the school could do. She wasn't doing anything you could catch her at, just words. If you said them in a normal voice, they sounded perfectly innocent. But she never said them in an innocent voice."

Rose nodded her head while Janet talked. "I remember," she said. "She would try her stuff with me when I started dating my husband. We met when he moved into our school during his senior year. She was trying to get his attention, but he had her number."

"Tammy was just like that in high school. The day Ryan showed up on her motorcycle, I saw Tammy watching her—well, watching all the boys watch her. She was relentless after that."

"I remember Jared coming home and telling me about the boys. They were asking him why you didn't talk and if you were a snob. I asked him once what he said to them." Annie and I were looking at her, waiting for her to finish her thought. Janet only took a bite of her muffin and sat there. When she did say something, it was about how good the muffin was and that she would need to ask Connie what she put in them.

"And," I said. "And what did he say?"

"Oh, he said that you were just quiet and to leave you alone, or else. He was quite happy the day they stopped trying to ask you out. He said something about them not being worthy of you."

I just sat there with my mouth hanging open. I was glad I had nothing in there because it would have fallen out. I always thought the boys gave up because I never answered them. I was in shock that they were talking to me, to begin with. I would look at them as they spoke to me. I would respond to what they said in my head, but I never said anything out loud. Annie would laugh at me after they finally gave up and walked away. It was the beginning of my nondating existence.

"It was after they stopped talking to me that Tammy stopped her endless harassment." Not that she stopped altogether. It always seemed like I was her favorite victim. She liked that I would freeze up and not respond. It felt like it took me forever to undo the damage those words did to me.

It was going to college that helped—being away from everything and being in a new environment, seeing new people, and learning new ways to cope. Annie was right there with me, still getting me into trouble. I kept going to therapy for a while after high school. The thing that helped most was a movie I watched one Saturday during my freshman year. If someone were to ask Annie about that movie, she would roll her eyes and start reciting dialogue. I watched it that many times.

The thing that helped me was watching how the main character interacted with people. They never seemed to answer questions, and when someone said something mean or stupid, he just looked at them.

He didn't have much of an expression. It was as though what the other character said had been dropped into a well. No response. No reaction. I practiced that look in the mirror. I also practiced it on Annie. She hated it. I had so many pillows thrown at me throughout our years as roommates.

When I'm forced to interact with Tammy, I pull out "the look," and she usually walks away. Not lately, though. She has been upping her game and trying to break me. At some point, she was going to have to stop.

"Are you even listening to me?" I tuned back into the conversation. I'd been lost in my thoughts.

"What did you say?"

"I said we had better get out of here."

"I looked up to see Becky come into the kitchen and glare at us.

"Right." I started packing everything up. I noticed that Annie had stuffed the leftover pastries in her bag.

"I saw that young lady." Janet took one of the muffins back, but left the cinnamon rolls.

"Sorry, Becky. We'll be out of your way in just a minute."

We were out the back door and in the alley when I realized Tammy could see us cross the road if she was still in the window seat.

"Don't worry about her. We'll distract her." Rose seemed to read my mind.

"Oh, this could be like that spy movie we watched the other night—the one where they distracted the bad guy by dumping their coffee in his lap," Janet said

"I don't think that would work. What about that other movie, the one with the really cute guy?"

We watched them walk off, talking about their plans for espionage.

"I think your aunts need to get out more. And I don't mean the movies."

Chapter 12

Braden

I spent the weekend with my grandparents. I hated leaving the morning after my date with Ryan. But when the people you love need you, you go. There had been a health scare with my grandfather. He was fine. But I stayed all weekend. Between my mother and me, we were able to get things in order at their house and keep my grandmother company at the hospital.

Pulling into the high school's parking lot, I found my usual spot taken. Typical Monday. I made it to my classroom without running into the principal or the secretary. I saw Stan lurking by his door, watching for me. I subtly waved my hand at him as I went past.

There had been some issue on Friday when I wasn't there, something so important that it required a staff meeting. The last time we had an emergency staff meeting, it was over someone using the copy machine excessively. Since the administration didn't know who it was, we all had to sit through a twenty-minute lecture on the proper use of the copier and conservation of paper. The fact that there were handouts on paper waste created by the printer and using the precious paper did not escape our notice or our ridicule in the meeting texts.

"What's the meeting about this time," I asked Stan as he slipped in my door.

"There was a food fight in the cafeteria on Friday. Not sure who started it, but I know who finished it."

"And." I motioned to him to continue.

"It was a new girl. She just started last week. I think that the hijinks of the football team, the ones who started it, got a little out of control. It all ended when she mashed a milk carton on one of the players' heads and then rubbed chocolate cake on his face. Not only that, she then proceeded to pick up her stuff and walk out."

"That doesn't seem like enough to start a cafeteria-wide food fight."

"It wasn't cafeteria-wide. Just the football players. The one who wore cake and milk was the one who started it. He also may have gotten a little overzealous and hit the new girl with something. The whole thing was over in minutes."

"Wow. Anyone record it?"

"Of course." Stan pulled out his phone, pressed some things, and then handed me the phone.

There it was in full color, though on a small screen. Yup, she got nailed in the back of the head. It was obvious by the shocked look on the boy's face that he had not expected that. And there she went. Pouring the milk and smashing the cake.

"Wow," I said again. "That was impressive." I handed the phone back. "Why are we having the meeting?"

"I think that the principal wants us to understand the intense wrongness of food fights. I am prepared to hear about world hunger and famine. The principal always reminds me of my grandmother. She always said things like that when I was growing up. Never understood the correlation."

I looked at the clock and saw that we only had a few minutes to get there. "The meeting had better be short; classes start soon. We'd better get going."

The meeting went about as expected. World hunger was mentioned, as was famine. Fluid was mentioned a mere twelve times. We were counting any form of the word now.

I scrolled back through my texts and laughed quietly at some of the comments. In person, Stan is very quiet and jumpy. Put a keyboard in front of the man, and he has snark and humor for days.

I was just putting my phone away when a piece of paper landed on my desk in front of me. I looked up, and there was the girl from the video.

"Hi. Can I help you?"

"I got transferred to your English class." I looked at the paper she handed me while she looked around the room.

"Was there a problem with your other English class?"

"They said I needed to be in this one. They didn't give me a reason."

"Huh, well, find a seat."

"Are they assigned?" She looked around the room. Her eyes darted from the door to the empty seats.

"No, just take one."

I looked at the paper she had given me. Under the reason for transfer, it just said teacher request. I would need to look into that. She seemed like a reasonable person. I probably would have put cake in the guy's face, too.

It was just at that moment and right before he walked through the door that I remembered the guy in question was in this class as well. I quickly looked around to see where she was sitting. It was right next to where the football player sat.

I had barely opened my mouth to suggest another seat when the young man in question came through the door. Took one look at the girl sitting next to his chair and smiled. When she saw him coming, her reaction was not quite as joyful.

To head off any conversations, I quickly started the roll call. I added the new girl, Gina, to the role. It was the beginning of a new marking period and the office had given me a new roll sheet. When I got to one of the names, I stopped and reread it. I could tell by the expression on his face that the owner of the name knew it was coming. I couldn't remember why I hadn't made the connection earlier in the year.

"Gilbert Blythe," I looked twice at the name.

"Here, and I go by Gill." I knew that. I should probably have remembered and used the name I had been calling him all year.

Gina turned toward him. "Are you serious? That's your name?"

"Yes, do you have a problem with it?"

"Is your girlfriend's name Anne by any chance?"

"I don't have a girlfriend."

"Okay, your parents have a seriously strange sense of humor."

I barely heard his response, "Tell me about it."

I finished calling the roll and noticed some of the kids starting to pull their phones out. "Phones away. How many people have their reading book from the library? Has anyone finished their first one?"

A few hands went up for the second question, and most went up for the first.

"Gill, can you explain to Gina about the books? Thanks." I have often found that not giving them a chance to respond negatively usually got the job done.

Starting the discussion on the day's writing topic moved everyone in the right direction. I couldn't wait to tell Ryan about all of this. It had been way too long since I had seen her.

The day moved along at the usual speed. Slow. I decided to walk to the library after school instead of driving.

I managed to get out of the building before anyone could grab me to talk. Lately, it seemed like everyone wanted to talk about something with me right after school. If not students, then other faculty. Thinking about that reminded me I needed to find Gina's last teacher and find out what had brought about the schedule change. I could think of no way the previous food fight would have been a cause, but you never could tell with some teachers. I had noticed that the teacher in question had been there since before my time and was considered by most to be the least user-friendly. I turned around and went back inside to find the teacher in question.

When I made it back out into the sunshine, I breathed in the warm air. I was right. She got transferred because of the food fight. The teacher didn't want to take a chance on problems. I pointed out that she hadn't had any problems all year. She just stared at me without saying anything. The walk and the fresh air would help clear that conversation out of my head.

I stopped at the corner and looked across the street at the library. A few kids were sitting outside at the table, and a couple more on the steps. I noticed one older woman hesitate before she started up the steps. She looked around at the teens before taking the first cautious step.

I hurried across the street to see if she needed any help. Before I could get there, a young woman went to her side. I had seen her hurrying up the sidewalk across the street toward the library.

"Hey, Gramma, let me hold that." Gina reached out and took the bag from the woman's hand and replaced it with her hand. I noticed the older woman smile and pull Gina's hand closer. "I thought you were going to wait for me?"

"I thought maybe you had already gone inside." She still looked nervously at the teens on the steps.

I slowed down so that I could observe without getting in the way. I didn't notice Gil coming up behind me until he went by.

"Excuse me, Mr Mitchel." He made it to the steps and started herding the recalcitrant teens off the steps and directing them to the bench. "You're blocking the steps. People can't get up."

"We're sitting to the side." One of the girls complained.

"Yeah, but what if someone needs to hold the handrails to get up the stairs?" He motioned to Gina and her grandmother as they finally started up the stairs. The others turned to look.

"Oh, good point. Sorry," she said to Gina's grandmother.

The steps cleared fairly quickly. Gil was just about to head up the stairs when he stopped and watched Gina go through the door.

"Everything okay," I asked.

"Sure. What's up with the new girl? You know anything?"

"Not anything I could share with you."

"Are teachers under HIPAA as well?"

"No."

"I just wondered about her. See you later, Mr. Mitchel." He headed up the steps and into the library.

I followed him up the steps. I couldn't wait to tell Ryan about my day. I only hoped hers had been as good.

Chapter 13

Ryan

Frank had been only mildly upset by the changes. It was good having him back, but I missed having the office to hide in. After the past week, I now understand why Frank kept the door mostly closed. Only open enough to hear us at the desk if there was an issue. Which usually involved Tammy giving me a hard time, or the Book Club getting out of control.

The morning session of the book club did, in fact, get out of control. There was a larger-than-usual disagreement about the book. In this case, the ending. It was not a happy ending. The book ended along the lines of Hamlet. Everyone died. The diehard Agatha Christie fans were okay with that. They had no problem with the ending at all. The other part of the group preferred to have everything neatly tied up, and the bad guy getting what was coming to them, while the detective, or at least someone, had a happy ending. Muffins were thrown.

When Frank came out of his office, Annie had lost the Rock, Paper, Scissors, and was about to go in and try to settle the argument.

"I'll handle this," he said as he pushed the glasses back up on his nose and straightened his sweater.

We both watched as he headed off to the conference room, looking like a marshal about to square off with the bank robbers in a western.

"Do you think he's going to make it out alive?" Annie leaned her forearms on the counter next to me, as we watched Frank head off to his possible demise.

"Sure, none of those women want to face Marge if anything happens to him." Frank's wife, Marge, was scary. Not only was she in charge of the building's maintenance, but she was also the head of the library board. No one messed with her. She knew everything about everyone. She even knew more gossip than the book club. I always thought she should have been at least in the book club. Janet finally explained to me why she wasn't a part of that select group.

Back when they were all in elementary school together, Marge and Janet were friends. They were still friends, just not best friends. That is too much leadership for one friendship. Both of them had strong personalities even then. It was decided that they should never be in the same group at the same time, though they both had something to do with the library. Neither invaded the other's space unless it was absolutely necessary.

Like the time the library board was trying to hire someone to replace the prior head librarian from somewhere else, passing over Frank. Something that was not going to be taken lightly by the book club and other patrons. A covert campaign headed by Janet and backed up by Marge was started.

One by one, the library board came to their senses about promoting Frank. It was whispered, though never proved, that the book club visited every member of the hiring committee. The committee members kept a low profile for several weeks after Frank's promotion. The information that was shared with them has long been guessed at by both Annie and me. Neither Marge nor Janet will confirm or deny our guesses.

As we watched Frank head off to his possible demise, Annie handed me her phone.

"Did you know there is a Book Club group text?"

"What?" I looked down at her phone, and sure enough, there was a group text. And it was flying. Not only were the ladies yelling at each other, but they were also casting dispersions about each other by text.

"You know darn well, Frank, that this book club is not a nuisance."

I recognized my Aunt's voice as Frank closed the door behind him. As usual, Frank used his quiet indoor voice. The voices within the room quieted, but the texts were getting louder and louder—or they would have if they had volume.

"Oh, my, can she say that?" Even my cheeks flamed at the text.

"Wow, I did not think your aunt was both that eloquent and able to take someone apart by text."

We heard the door start to open and looked up. Annie put her phone out of sight, but it no sooner opened than closed again. The quiet arguing went on for another fifteen minutes.

We both jumped when the library door was yanked open. We looked to see Marge come through and head straight to the conference room. We looked around and noticed that Florie's daughter, Michelle, was sitting at one of the tables.

She shrugged before mouthing, "I thought Frank might need backup." She held up her phone as well.

"Are you in the text group as well?" Annie crossed the room so she could whisper. I followed right behind her.

"I put myself on. My mother knows since she saw my name, but after this, I might get kicked out."

We all turned to look at the door and then down at the phones. The texts had stopped. And the shouting had stopped.

"Do you think they're all still alive," I asked.

Annie and Michelle both shrugged. I was starting to walk towards the door when we heard laughter. Everyone in the library gave a collective sigh and went back to what they had been doing. Both Annie and Michele looked down at their phones.

A few minutes later, Frank and Marge both came out of the room. She kissed Frank's cheek before heading towards the door. She paused and looked around before waving at Michelle. Michelle tentatively waved back.

"I'll be leaving soon. I'm having lunch with Marge, and I might be a little longer than usual." He looked at both of us as if daring us to say anything. Neither of us said a word. He closed the door behind him as he went into his office.

"That was interesting."

"Yup," Annie said, popping the p.

The rest of the book club came out of the room shortly after and headed for the door. Janet and Rose both waved at me as they went by. Michelle stood up and headed out the door with her mother. She nodded her head at us and waved her phone.

"I think we need a book club family member support group text," Annie said.

"You don't have any family in the book club," I said.

"I am vicariously attached through you. We are as close as sisters, so that makes me family."

"Good point."

The rest of the day was uneventful. I had received a text from Braden saying he would come by the library after school let out. After I got the text, the day that had been flying past seemed to grind to a standstill. Every time I looked at the clock, expecting it to be at least an hour later, I saw only a few minutes had gone by.

When the students started trickling in, I started to get antsy. Where before I was impatient, I was now much more—well, more impatient.

I was a little concerned by my response to Braden coming back into my life. Yes, I had known *of* him in high school. We had some great conversations on the phone, getting to know each other better. But I still felt like things, or I should say feelings, were moving a little too fast. My experiences with men in the past had not gone well. They were either chased off by my awkwardness or by my anxiety. The two often seemed to go hand in hand.

The previous night, I had tossed and turned most of the night, overthinking my relationship. Trying to predict what would finally drive him away. I knew that that was not logical thinking. But sometimes my logical brain was not in control. Especially after midnight.

I watched as the door opened and a woman entered the library. I assumed the young woman with her was her granddaughter by the way they were walking hand in hand. I watched as the girl found a comfortable spot for the older woman and went to look at the book display.

A young man I knew to be on the football team came in after them. He stopped to watch the direction the girl went and then followed her. He stopped beside her at the display and started talking. I would have continued to try to eavesdrop, except the door opened again. Turning to see who had come in the door. I saw Braden.

I watched him walk toward me—a smile on his face.

"Hello."

"Hello, yourself. How's your grandfather?"

"My mother said he was doing well. He and my grandmother both kicked my mother out this morning and sent her home." He looked over his shoulder at the two-by-the-book display. "She's new. Have you met her?"

"No, I think this is the first time she's come to the library. I have seen the woman who came in with her, though. She was in last week. She didn't get a library card, so I didn't learn her name."

Annie came up from behind us and joined the conversation. "Isn't that the two students in the food fight video?"

"What video?" I went toward Annie, who was already doing something with her phone.

"This video." She handed me her phone, and I watched the video with the sound off. When it was over, I looked at the two standing by the books.

"Well, the animosity seems to have lessened a little." I watched as the two standing near each other moved a little closer. They were picking up and talking about the books.

"I never made the connection before, but did you know his name is the same as the young man in *Anne of Green Gables,"* Braden asked.

"You just figured that out?" Annie smiled at Braden. "Oh, sorry. I forgot you've been gone for a little while. Ever since that poor kid was little, he's been teased about it. It's a wonder he hasn't already made plans to change it." Annie put her phone away.

"He won't. He's named after his mother's father, and Gil really loves him. It is an unfortunate pairing of names." I reached under the counter to get a library card form.

"What's the girl's name?" Annie used her chin to point at the pair.

"Gina."

"Oh, thank goodness. They would never have lived it down if it had been Anne."

I was starting to move out from behind the counter to go and talk to the older woman when the day went from good to bad with the opening of the door.

Chapter 14

Ryan

I felt my fingers start to tingle when I saw Tammy enter the library. My face started to feel like ice shards were pricking at my skin. I reached under the counter and grasped the ledge that the counter sat on, trying to focus on the tactile feeling of the wood and not the way my stomach was bottoming out.

Usually, the anxiety didn't start to ratchet up until after she started talking. Her incessant attacks were taking a greater toll than I had realized. If the bodily sensation of the attack were coming on this strongly, so quickly.

Braden looked behind him and noticed Tammy. He was just starting to turn toward her when Gill reached him with a question. Braden followed him over to the books. He kept looking at me, trying to gauge how I was doing.

I felt someone tugging at the back of my shirt. I moved away from the counter as Tammy reached it. Annie stepped in front of me to talk to her.

"Can I help you?"

"I need to ask Ryan a question about a book she recommended last week." Once she made eye contact with me, she did not break it. I looked away, but I knew she was still staring.

At the precise moment I felt I was going to have to talk to her, Frank came out of his office. His Tammy radar was impeccable.

"Oh, hello, Tammy." He gave her a cursory wave. Turning to me, he said. "Ryan, can you come in here for a minute? I need you to show me what orders were placed while I was gone. " He kept talking as he turned to go into his office. I followed behind him. Giving a small wave to Tammy as if to say, "Sorry, I'm busy."

The door closed behind me. Frank had been waiting for me to come through.

He didn't close it all the way and moved to peer through the crack.

"What happened with her while I was gone?"

"She came in every day from Monday through Saturday. She followed me around doing her usual tricks. Asking me to find a book she was already holding, and complaining." I tried to look through the crack as well, but he elbowed me out of the way.

"What brought all this on? Usually, she limits her visits to once a week."

"Did you see the man I was talking with?" He turned away from the crack to look at me. "He's the new teacher at the school this year. The one you were supposed to do the display for." I looked at him with a raised eyebrow.

"Right, sorry about that. I got distracted and forgot to let you know. You did a good job, though."

"Thanks. Anyway, I went out with him last week, and Tammy has been in attack mode ever since."

"You went out on a date? That's great." Then, more to himself, he said, "I wonder if Marge knows?"

I then went on to tell him about hiding out in the bakery and my other encounters with her in the library. Until I finally did something and stood up for myself, she was going to keep picking at me.

There was more talking at the desk, and we both looked through the crack in the door. There was a little window in the door. But we knew from experience that it was obvious when someone moved the curtain to see out of it. I tried anyway. I moved the tiniest corner to see what was happening.

Tammy was talking to Annie and happened to be looking at the door. She saw my curtain movement. And said with a really loud voice.

"Ryan, I really need to ask you something. You can come out of hiding now. I see you."

Surprisingly, it was Frank who opened the door.

"Is there a problem? I could hear you talking in my office with the door closed. If I want to check and see who is out here, that is my prerogative. If you don't need anything, perhaps you could move so the people behind you can be helped."

With that, he closed the door all the way. Neither of us waited to see what would happen. I quickly moved out of his way and went to sit in the one chair available to me.

"That woman. She has been like that since birth. Her and her mother. I always dreaded having to deal with both of them during story-time. Her mother's constant complaints about the lack of truly educational opportunities for her daughter at the library. I mean, really, who does she think she is?" He leaned back in his chair, looking up at the ceiling.

With a sigh, he continued, "Luckily, that younger one has some sense. I really did have a few questions for you. But Marge is going to be back to get me for lunch." He picked up his jacket and moved towards the door. "You can stay in here for a few minutes longer, just to be sure."

"No, I'd better go out there. I wanted to ask Braden something."

We both went out the door at the same time. Marge had barely made it through the door when she stopped and turned to go back out. Frank hurried his steps to catch up to her. It may have seemed to outsiders looking in that she dominated him. We knew that wasn't true. You could tell by the shy smile she gave him when he held the door and took her hand. Her personality may have been louder than his, but their relationship was very equal.

I had made it to my desk before Tammy was back. The woman is relentless.

"I need you to show me where that book on Greek basketry is. The one you showed me last week. I think I need it."

I reached for a piece of paper while I entered the search terms into my computer. After I found what I was looking for, I wrote it down. I turned and walked back to her, handing her the piece of paper. "Here is the call number. You can find it in the nonfiction section upstairs."

"I need you to show me," she said with her fake smile.

"I'm sorry. I need to help the people behind you. It is right up at the top of the stairs." Would I have normally gone to get it to help someone? Probably. Tammy, no.

"I'm not sure I know where the section is." Her smile was so syrupy that I could feel my teeth start to ache.

"I can help you." Annie snatched the paper out of her hand and started walking off."

"Oh, thank you, I'll wait here. My legs are killing me from my workout this morning."

"All the more reason to walk it off." Annie had paused and was waiting for Tammy. Both women continued to stare at each other. "This is a limited-time offer. Either I help you now, or you find it yourself."

Tammy gave an audible huff as she walked off. She couldn't back down from her request. People were starting to stare. And though she didn't mind people staring at her victim. She did not like to be the center of that level of curiosity.

I reached out to the next person in line, Tammy's sister.

"I'm sorry. I have no idea how I managed to be born into my family. I guess I'm more like my Dad." She handed me one of the books from the display.

"Oh," I said, "I think you are going to enjoy this one. I did."

Her smile lit up her face. She was already beautiful, and her smile made it more evident. "Did you? What other books do you recommend from the shelf?" She turned her body so she faced the shelf. I couldn't see the book titles from where we were standing, but I could make out the general color and covers.

"There is one over there that is a gothic love story." I tapped the cover of the book she was checking out. "It is kind of like this one. I put a lot of my favorites on the shelf when Mr. Mitchel wasn't looking." I winked at her when she turned back.

"Thanks." She took the book and started back towards the shelves. Once there, she was back in conference with Gina and Gil, who were still talking. After a few furtive glances at me, they went back to looking at the books.

I was watching them, which let Braden sneak up on me. "Are you okay?" He reached out and touched my hand.

I noticed that there wasn't anyone waiting, so I moved around the counter.

"I am getting there. I know what she is going to say and how she is going to act, and it still gets to me every time. Or worse, I start panicking before she even says anything. It is almost Pavlovian. She shows up, and my anxiety starts. I have no idea how to reframe it. I know that it's what my therapist said to do. To just let it go. But I can't. My brain latches onto what she says, and I start to spiral down."

"I haven't had an anxiety attack. So I'm not sure exactly what it is that you go through. My grandfather had them. It was hard when I lived with him, because I didn't know what to do. I was just out of high school and had no empathy or understanding. It took me a little while. I talked with my grandmother and my mother about it. Not sure how much help I can give. But, I can be there for you."

"Thanks. Annie has it down to a science. I guess she'd have to after years of being my best friend."

"I have to go pick something up from the print shop before they close. Will you be okay till I get back?"

"Of course. We close the library at five." I wasn't sure if he was ready for my family's level of chaos. I took a chance anyway. "Would you like to come to a family cookout?"

"That sounds great."

"It's at my house. My Aunt and Uncle are having an anniversary, and I have the best grill. Everyone will be there. Annie, also."

He took my hand and squeezed it once before letting go. "I'll meet you there."

I watched him walk out the door. Suddenly, I felt more excited about a family gathering than I had in a long time.

I turned to see Annie coming back down with Tammy in tow. Neither of them looked happy.

"That wasn't the book you showed me last week. I couldn't remember the title, but I know it wasn't upstairs. You were over in that section. I think you'll have to find it after all."

I looked at Annie, who was fuming. I couldn't think of any way to get rid of her. Other than to go and find the stupid book on Greek baskets or whatever it was she was on about. The only book I know of was a fictional book with a Greek statue and a basket on the cover. Only Tammy would think it was a how-to book.

"I know the one, I'll get it for you. I'll be right back."

I hoped she would get the hint and wait. She did for all of two seconds before following me into the stacks. The venom started dripping as soon as we were far enough from the desk that she could casually whisper.

"I have no idea what you think you're doing. If my calves were that shape, I certainly wouldn't want my skirts that short. Are those new shoes? I thought they were maybe from your grandmother."

And on it went. When I think about what she says or write it down, I can see how small and petty it all is. When she starts talking in that tone and the endless nature of the comments, it really does start to feel like water torture.

By the time I had handed the book to Tammy and made my way back to the desk, I was losing feeling in my arms, and I could feel that need to run from the room. There is nothing as terrifying to me as the feeling that I am being chased by monsters or murderers, and all I am doing is standing still in the library with the sun from the windows shining on me.

I knew that my look was starting to get a little feral. When I looked over at Tammy to hand her the book, I saw a smug little smile on her face. At that moment, the anxiety I had been feeling paused. And I was filled with rage. Rage that this woman had been purposefully trying to get me to panic for her sheer enjoyment.

I turned toward the computer as though I were going to check it out. "Oh, you know what," I said as I pulled the book back towards myself. "This book should have been pulled from the shelves. Someone is waiting for it." I put the book back under the counter.

I knew from the past that not getting the book she wanted because someone else was waiting for it would make her angry.

I had a perverse sense of joy when I saw that smug little smile slip from her face.

"Why was it on the shelf then?"

"The request seems to have come in this morning. I hadn't checked the requests yet. Sorry."

There was, in fact, no request for the book. No one had checked this poor book out in a year. I don't think anyone even knew we still had it. But I was not going to give it to her. I have no idea how many library rules I just broke. All I know is it felt nice to have the upper hand for once.

Tammy leaned forward so that she was only a few inches away from me. "I know what you are doing. Trying to embarrass me in front of people. It won't work. You are still a nobody. Always will be." She leaned back and said louder than normal, "I hope they like the book.

Let me know when they return it. Now that I know the title, I'll be able to find it easier. Too bad you didn't know it at the beginning."

She left the library with her head held just as high as she usually did. Her sister hurried after her. "Unfortunately, she's my ride." She waved at the others and dashed out the door.

Once Tammy was gone, I turned and walked back towards Frank's office. I sat in the first chair I came to and put my head down. That didn't seem to help, so I stood up and started pacing back and forth, swinging my arms, trying to let some of the energy that was raging through my body out. The tingling in my arms was increasing.

"Breathe, Ryan. Breathe with me." Annie had my hands in one of hers and used the other to move my face so that I was looking directly at her. "Breath with me. Look in my eyes. No, don't look away. You are safe. Breathe."

I could feel my breathing start to slow down. I breathed with Annie. By looking in her eyes, I could focus on the right now.

"I've got you. You're safe."

I could feel my body start to come back to center. Though it was hard, the attack wasn't as bad as some of the others and had passed more quickly. I think the moment of rage that I experienced helped to minimize it.

We heard voices coming from the desk area. I looked out and saw Gina, Gil, and Gina's grandmother standing at the counter. They were directing people back to their seats or to just move a little bit farther from the desk while they waited. The three of them had taken over crowd control.

Annie held my hand for a second longer before she went out to the counter. "Thank you," I heard her say to the three of them.

"You are very welcome. I need to get a library card." I stepped out of Frank's office and saw the older woman talking to Annie. With a wink at me, she said. "I think I'll like a library that takes its hold list so seriously."

Annie started to laugh while she worked to get the information logged into the system.

I picked up some of the books that needed to be reshelved and headed into the safety of the stacks. It was soothing for me to put the books away. The sound they made as they slid onto the shelf eased some of the tension from my shoulders.

I was just about to round a corner and go down the next row when I nearly tripped over a pirate sitting on the floor. Esther was trying to tie his shoes.

"Oh, I'm sorry. I didn't see you there."

"That's okay. We are a little below eye level even for us." She always joked about her height. She was barely five feet.

When she was done, the pirate stood up and started towards the door. As Esther went past me, she patted my shoulder. "We think you're perfect."

And then they were gone. And my day was a little brighter. The only thing left for the day was introducing Braden to my family.

Chapter 15

Ryan

By the time Annie and I got to my house, the party was in full swing. Janet had used her key to get in and get things going.

The back porch had several tables set up with beautiful tablecloths. There were fairy lights strung up around the porch as well as out into the yard, and around the few tables that were set up. I knew from experience that a lot of the eating would be done in the house. My lack of furniture in the living room had come in handy before for parties.

When I moved into the house after college, I only brought a small amount of furniture I needed from the college dorms. My grandmother's furniture had gone to various people in the family. Things that they had an attachment to over the years. At first, Janet and Rose complained that I would need it. I explained to them that I didn't care, and it would give me a chance to make the house my own instead of a shrine for my grandmother.

I had slowly started to get pieces at yard sales and auctions. I was serious about wanting my own things to make the house more mine. It was taking time to fill a house with just what I wanted. Which meant that some of the rooms had very little in them. I spent most of my time in a comfortable chair reading, thus no couch. I did have a beautiful table in the kitchen. No table in the dining room. The rooms I felt most comfortable in were the ones that were filled. A four-bedroom house was a lot for one person.

The lack of furniture meant there was plenty of room for folding tables.

"Hey, girls!" Janet came down the few steps to wrap us in a hug. She gave Annie a quick hug with a kiss on the cheek. My hug lasted longer. Someone must have told her about the attack. "How are you?" She pulled away to look me in the eyes. "Was it a bad one?"

"I'm fine. It wasn't too bad. Annie was there."

She pulled back, not releasing me, and looked into my eyes. "Sometimes I just want to..."

She didn't finish the statement. Whatever it was, I knew it wasn't anything she would do, only something she wanted to do.

"What can we do?" Annie started into the house carrying the cookies she had brought.

I never brought anything to these things. I was always told it was because I was letting everyone invade. I knew the truth. No one wanted to risk my cooking. The joke was on them. I had spent the summer driving over to the next town and taking culinary classes for the inept. That was the actual name of the class. We met once a week. I could not only cook but also bake as well. Turns out that, like most things, I was overthinking everything.

"Rose, how are you?" I greeted my aunt with a hug and a squeeze. I noticed how she looked over my shoulder at Janet. Her unasked question must have been answered. She just squeezed me like a lemon and let go. "I asked Braden to come by; I hope that was okay?"

"Oh, definitely. Can't wait to meet him."

"Hey there, Ryan," Jason said as he came through the kitchen door. "We found this guy outside. Says he knows you." He stepped out of the way so I could see Braden coming in behind him.

I moved forward to greet him. "I'm so glad you came." I leaned in, hugging him. I think I took him by surprise. He was a little slow in returning it.

"Hello," he might have been slow to start, but when he caught up, he was all in. He pulled me close, pressing me against his chest.

I pulled away first, feeling the cold air move in between us. I hadn't realized how warm I had become hugging him. The warmth could have also come from my bright red cheeks.

When I turned to introduce him to my family, I felt a little off-kilter. Were hugs supposed to be that...? Words temporarily fled my mind when I tried to put a word to it.

"This is my aunt, Janet."

"It is nice to meet you."

"It is very nice to meet you, Braden. I have heard good things about you."

"Really?" Braden didn't look at me, but I felt his hand move to join mine. We had held hands before, but this, in front of my family, felt important.

"You know Jason," I motioned to my smirking cousin.

"How's it going," Jason asked.

"Good."

We moved on to the others in the family until I was sure he was completely confused and would never remember anyone. I left him at the grill, talking to one of my uncles. By the sounds of things, they had people in common. Not surprising considering the size of the town.

My aunt cornered me in the kitchen as I reached into the refrigerator for a cold drink.

"There are drinks in the sink with the ice." She pointed at the sink in question. And sure enough, there was enough of a variety of beverages to suit anyone. Due to the number of children running around, none of the drinks were alcoholic. That way, the kids could just grab, and no one had to worry about what they were drinking.

My extended family had lots of children. Janet was my aunt through marriage. And Rose was my mother's sister. The family tree started getting confusing after a certain point, and we just called each other family.

"What?" I turned away from the sink with my favorite soda in my hand.

"He seems nice," Rose said.

"He is."

The conversation stalled at that point. She was looking around at the family moving through, and I was bracing for whatever comment was heading my way.

"I heard about this afternoon. Are you okay?"

"I'm okay. A little tired." I was always more tired after an attack. Having that much adrenaline running through my body always wore me out. "I'm hoping this get-together gives me some energy." Being with family always calmed me, and that gave me more energy. Maybe not the kind that lets me go for a run, but the kind that helps me feel grounded.

"I do too."

Janet chose that moment to join her best friend and partner in crime. The two of them personified the adage of the one you called when you needed to bury a body. There was nothing they wouldn't do for each other.

"Did you ask her yet?" Janet nudged Rose.

"No, I haven't had a chance. We were just discussing this afternoon."

"Sometimes, I just want to," she didn't finish that sentence. In the past, she would say she was too much of a lady to say what she wanted. But once she hit fifty, that filter left the building. Now I think it had more to do with being incriminated in any crimes.

Rose patted her arm. "I know, we are working on the problem, remember."

"Oh, right." The smile they shared would be enough to scare a lesser person. I had been in on enough of their plans to be worried enough to remember who the family lawyer was.

"Do you think," Janet was interrupted by Jared coming into the room, asking a question.

He had a child on his back and one hanging off his leg. "Dad wants to know if you have all the meats ready; he wants to start cooking."

"Yes, just a minute," Janet moved to the refrigerator and took out the platter I had previously seen. "Tell him to cook the chicken first, it takes longer, and then the other stuff." She tried to hand him the plate but realized he had no hands. With a sigh, she went to take it outside.

"Rose, keep her right there till I get back."

"Okay," Rose turned to me and smiled. It was the type of smile that usually made me worried.

"Glad I'm not you," Jared said as he started to limp off with the children attached to him.

I looked at Rose again. She still stood there with a smile. I go to move around her, and she moves. "We only need about five minutes. That's it." Rose was using her pleading voice. The one she used on me when I was little and trying to get into something I shouldn't have. It was almost as good as one of Annie's pouts for getting me to do something.

"I want to go find out if Braden is still alive." It was a flimsy response. And Rose knew it.

"He's fine," Janet said as she rejoined us. "They're talking about something out there. I didn't stop long enough to find out what it was." Turning to me, she gave the same slightly unhinged smile Rose had started with. Before the pleading one.

"I suppose you noticed the dust-up at the book club. Well, we have a problem, and we need your help." She looked over at Rose for confirmation.

"Right, we need your help. We need more members, younger members or older, doesn't matter. We just need more members. And you might know who we can ask to join."

I sighed inwardly. For all I knew, I was going to be either the getaway driver in a heist or the lookout. With those two, it could be anything.

"I could probably come up with a few names. What are you looking for?" Knowing those two, they could be looking for anything.

"We need people who read, obviously." Rose nodded at Janet to show her agreement.

"Do you read the books your group picks out," I asked.

"Mostly. Right, Rose?"

"Oh, definitely."

Those two definitely did not read the books. I know because I have heard some of their arguments. And those are mostly centered on the end or the beginning.

"I saw someone today. I think they might be a good match. They just got a library card, so I can check and talk to them the next time they come in. How many are you looking for?"

"I think we need about two more. Right, Janet?"

"Three."

"Why are you two trying to get an odd number?" There was something cagey about the two of them.

"We need to make sure there is a tie breaker. If we have an even number of people, then we could end up with a deadlock, and then what would we do? There would be anarchy and chaos."

"There is anarchy and chaos now. What were you arguing about this time?"

"The usual. Florie wants us to read a mystery her nephew wrote. I might be okay with it, but then she said, and she looked right at me when she said it, that we would need to promise to read the book. She said it like I don't read books. I read books all the time. I read two or three books a week." She looked around, checking to see who was listening. "I have trouble reading books people tell me to read. I don't like being told what to do."

I burst out laughing. I couldn't help it. The way she admitted to this took me so by surprise that I couldn't hold it in. Everyone knew Janet didn't like to be told what to do. It needed to be a request to her better nature. I couldn't stop laughing. Especially when I thought of all the times I had seen her completely ignore someone telling her to do something. The more I thought about it, the more I laughed.

"This is not funny. I don't know why you think this is funny." I could tell the laughing might be hurting her feelings.

"It isn't funny, not really. Sorry." I dried my eyes. Lowering myself onto a seat at the table, I brought myself under control. "Are you going to read the book. It would probably make her very happy since she is proud enough of her nephew to recommend his book."

"We will. It won't be for a few months. We need to get the book, and then she said he would come to the meetings if we read his book."

"I think she said she would force him to come if we read the book," Rose said.

"That sounds great. Have I read his books?" I asked.

"I don't know if you have, but I know Annie has. She reads every one of his books. I know she reads them before she puts them on the shelf. She is such a fast reader; she gets it done before you even have a chance to process the book."

"Oh, you mean Michael Johnson?" I whispered the name, looking around for Annie. She would sit and tell me everything about the books if I didn't stop her. She was nowhere to be seen, thankfully. "That would be great."

The back door opened, and I heard my cousins Jared and Jason coming down the hall. I could also hear Braden.

"Hey, Ryan. They need more ice for the ice chest. They said you knew where it was." Jared and Jason looked way too pleased with themselves about this request. I knew the reason why; they had been waiting for this for a long time.

"When I come back up, you two and I are going to have a long talk about my nonexistent dating life in high school."

Jared reached out and took my hand. "I thought you knew."

Jason stood by his brother, uniting them even in the face of a potential threat. "You know that none of those guys was really worthy of you."

"That is a choice I should have been able to make. I missed opportunities to get to know them."

"With your anxiety, would you have really been able to go on a date and not panic? We wanted to save you from further fodder for bullies."

"Even if that was true. You took the opportunity away from me." I sighed before turning away. "You are right. It would have given Tammy more to torture me with. But then again. I might have met someone who could have helped me and become a friend."

"We are sorry that it hurt you. But we would probably do it again," Jared said.

I looked at them, wondering if they had in fact done it again. They both looked away and started talking to Rose.

"How much ice do you need?

"A couple of bags. Right, Jared?"

"Yup, that should do it." They both looked suspicious. I already knew what they were planning.

Chapter 16

Ryan

I keep the ice in the big freezer in the basement. Jason and Jared have been trying to lure me down into the basement for a long time. And finally, the opportunity presented itself. I am very aware of why they are trying to get me down there. I decided to play along with them to get this over with.

"Sure, let me go get it."

"Do you need any help?" Braden moved to go with me, but Jared cut him off.

"Hey, did I show you Ryan's artwork?" I couldn't believe he was using that as a ploy.

"I got it. I'll be right back." I turned the light on at the switch outside the basement door. When I reached the bottom, I waited a few seconds before moving toward the freezer.

The door finished closing at the top of the stairs right before the lights went out. I could hear Jared laugh just before the door shut. I waited a breath before yelling out, "Hey!"

I reached out and turned on the light. I had had a switch installed at the bottom of the stairs just for this type of situation.

When we were all younger, before I moved in with them, I had shut the lights off on them when they were in the basement. I had been timed perfectly. My grandmother asked them to get some things for her. I knew she would ask them to do it that afternoon because I overheard her talking on the phone with Janet. When they arrived at the house, I started regaling them with all the ghost stories I knew.

All of them involved either the attic or the basement. These locations were important since I knew they would be moving things from the attic to the basement. The washing machine was in the basement, and our grandmother wanted to wash the clothes in the boxes before she donated them.

The yearly purge was at hand. My grandmother prepared for this with precision, organization, and lists. The lists were of all the things that we weren't using or rarely used. She would make the lists at the beginning of Spring. If we needed them or used the things on the list, she would cross them off. At the beginning of the following Spring everything that was left on the list would be donated.

I waited till the last trip down the stairs. I had been making little noises when they were down there. Kicking a small rock down the stairs when they weren't looking. Little things to get them on edge. The last trip down was when I brought it all together.

To be clear. This was actually revenge for their last prank. I was not this mean without reason. Over the Christmas break, we went skating. They had waited till I was skating with a guy I had been crushing on for the past year. When the couples skate started I was so excited and surprised when he asked me to skate with him. I knew it wasn't the big romantic gesture I had hoped for when I saw that it was a choice between Tammy and me. Come to think of it, that was probably the defining moment of her antagonism. As we skated around the rink, my little heart swelled with romantic dreams. And then Jared skated by us. He winked at me. Then Justin went past and winked as well.

The second time they went by, Jared said in a loud voice, "She's in love with you, man." I thought I would die of embarassment.

Justin went by next. His contributing comment was, "A lot."

I then understood why my diary was in a different place the day before. They had found it and read it.

I could feel the red move from the top of my head down to my toes. I would probably melt the ice I was giving off so much heat. He dropped my hand, and we skated to the edge as the music changed.

He turned to me, and I noticed that his face was just as red. He didn't even look at me when he said, "I don't like you like that." He then wandered off and did not even acknowledge me again. Tammy smirked at me, having heard the exchange.

I didn't stay for the rest of the skating time. I called my grandmother to come get me.

When the time came for revenge, I was ready. The pain and misery of that moment burned in me as I quietly shut the door and turned off the basement light.

The screams were magnificent.

My grandmother scolded me for scaring them, but she didn't turn on the light. She did crack the door so they could at least make it up the stairs. She had been the one to wipe away my tears and help me feel better. She called Janet, and the two of them were grounded until they were adults. Which, in reality, was about two weeks.

The look on their faces when they came up was worth all the trouble I might have gotten into. After that, I had been very careful never to go downstairs when they were at the house. When I moved back in, I had an electrician come out and put a switch for the lights at the bottom of the stairs. That way, I could turn the lights on or off at either end of the stairs.

I turned off the lights when I got to the top of the stairs. My cousins were standing at the top of the stairs, waiting for me to scream and make a dramatic arrival. Instead, I handed them the bag of ice and went back to the table.

"Did she just turn off the lights," Jasred asked.

"She did," Jason replied. Both cousins went to the still-open door and turned the lights on and then off. "Okay," they said at the same time, "How did you do that?"

"Take the ice out, and then we'll tell you." Rose shoved Jared out the door.

"We have been waiting twelve years to be able to do that. We planned it out in advance." Jason waited by the door for his brother's return.

Braden came and sat next to me. "I am so confused."

"Once long ago, in retaliation for a prank they pulled, I shut them down there without a light."

"After she set us up with ghost stories that she just happened to be reading. And then, we later found out, had made a lot of small noises and then asked if we had heard them. She had us so primed by the time she turned off the light that we almost had heart attacks." Jason paced away from the door and then back, looking out the window when he returned.

"I waited till you were on the last load into the basement before I did it, though."

"Probably because you knew that you would have to be the one doing the hauling if we outright refused."

Jared came running back into the room. "What did I miss?"

"You didn't miss anything," his mother said.

"When I moved in, I had another switch installed at the bottom."

"What? Why didn't we ever notice it?" Jason moved to the basement door, opening it and turning on the light so he could see the bottom of the stairs. "How did we not notice that?" He moved out of the way so his brother could look.

"That was tricky." They both looked at me with a new respect. Leading me to believe that there would be a new payback coming.

"We are now even." I tried to see if I could slide past them.

"We are so not even. That was a defining moment of my life, and I refuse to allow it to go unchallenged." I didn't think Jared would let it go.

"Fine."

"Hey, in there! The meat is done, someone come get it and set the rest of the things up."

"Coming." Janet and Rose both hit my cousins on the way by them.

"This is not over." Jason did his typical 'I'm watching you' motion.

I laughed and started to get up. Braden put out a hand to keep me at the table.

"Your family is not what I imagined. Well, partly it is. Your cousins are just as I remembered them. I didn't realize I knew one of your Uncles."

"They can be overwhelming."

"Also protective. How many uncles do you have?"

"My uncle Jake, my mother's brother, Janet's husband. My uncle Rory, Rose's husband. All the others are relatives of Rose's husband or Janet's family. Most here today are from Janet's family. She had five brothers. And they each had two or three children. Three of those children are married with children. Thus, the little rugrats are running around. I am not technically related to them, but I feel part of them." I smiled at the little one making off with one of Annie's cookies.

"That is quite the family. I am the only child of only children."

"Why did you say protective earlier? I know Jared and Jason are protective, but..." I didn't finish the statement. I was hoping he would fill in the blanks for me.

"Let's just say that I have been told by no fewer than six people that I am being watched as to my behavior with you."

"Were any of those six Jared and Jason?"

"No, actually, they were your uncles. And one aunt that I didn't get a name for, but she motioned towards the house and then made a slashing movement with her finger. I am not certain, but how I treat you might determine the length of my life."

"Everyone became very protective of me after my mom died. Especially when I was struggling so much with depression and anxiety. "

"It's nice. I'm glad you are so well loved."

A small hand landed on my leg. I looked down to see one of the many children who were running around the party.

Looking first at me, then at Braden, the little one said, "My mom wants to know if this guy is bothering you?"

I couldn't keep the laughter out of my voice when I replied, "No, he's my friend.'

The little girl looked Braden over, and with a "Hmm," she walked away.

The rest of the evening went well. I watched as Braden interacted with my cousins. He got sucked into a game of basketball in the driveway. With the porch and garage lights on, they had enough light to play. There wasn't enough light to accurately judge the fouls, however. I did warn him that fouls were only called on account of blood. Braden seemed to hold his own. Jared and Jason had him on their team. I was a little less worried about them roughing up their team member.

I was sitting on the steps that led to the kitchen door when Rose sat down next to me. "You like him."

"I think I do. I haven't seen him in a while, and then, wham, he's back in my life. It seems very sudden."

"Did you know him in high school?"

"Yes, and no. I knew who he was enough to have a small crush on him, but not enough to actually call him a friend or anything. And at the time could probably have told you his name if you asked. When he stopped to help me with the bee, I was surprised. I hadn't thought about him in a long time."

"You get along well together. You haven't done anything awkward or had any issues with your anxiety since he got here, not that you had any before he got here. I like him. Your uncles like him. He held his own in their grilling. Someone knows his mother. Family is important."

"I know. I'm not sure what I would have done without all of you backing me up through the years."

"You're easy to love, Ryan." She bumped my shoulder with hers before putting her arm around me. "Now what are we going to do about that pest that keeps bothering you?"

"I wish I knew. I stood up to her, sort of, today. She went through this whole thing about a book, then I lied and said that someone had it on hold. I'll have to check it out for her at some point if she asks again. I need to let Frank know about it so he doesn't accidentally tell on me."

"Frank has her number. Always has. Her mother is the same way. She once tried to ruin Frank and Marge's relationship way back when."

"What happened?" I hadn't ever heard this story. "I always thought Frank and Marge had been together since preschool."

Rose snorted, "Maybe not that long. But close." She drew in a breath and then yelled at her son to play nice. "It was in high school, as are most of the crazy things we do. Brenda, Tammy's mother, got insulted by Marge. Shocking, I know. Only she took things seriously. She started trying to hang around Frank. Always showing up at his locker. Trying to sit next to him in class. That sort of thing."

"Did she have a crush on him or something?"

"Oh, no. Nothing like that. She just wanted to hurt Marge. She didn't take into account that Frank loved Marge more than anything. And there was no getting him into a compromising situation. He would get up and move if she sat too close. Or he would start a conversation with someone and shut her out. He was wise to her. As was Marge. Back then, Marge was even smaller than she is now. She was downright tiny. She isn't very tall, and she has a nice figure now. Back then, she ran track and did gymnastics. That girl was strong and strong-willed. Frank was at every one of her meets, cheering her on. Anyway. Marge got wind of what Brenda was doing and got angry."

Rose paused again to yell at one of her sons. Then she yelled to one of her daughter-in-laws that she had something that would get the blood out of a shirt.

"Where was I, oh yeah, anyways, we talked to Marge, and then we just made sure that Frank wasn't alone. One day, Frank had had enough and told her that she was wasting her time and to leave him alone. He was really mad. Marge was across the room, and Brenda kept trying to hold his hand. Everyone in the cafeteria heard him. Brenda got up and stomped out. She has never forgiven Frank or Marge for that, even though it was totally her own fault."

"Tammy is relentless. I don't know how to counter that."

"I don't know either. I think you'll find a way to get her to back down. I heard she keeps trying to get Braden to pay attention to her. Like mother, like daughter."

She patted my leg and then got up, stretching and grimacing as she did.

"Are you heading out?" I looked around to see who was left.

"We are. I just need to round up my husband. The rest of them are on their own. I don't miss herding children." She kissed me on the top of my head before she went in to gather her husband and dishes.

I was still watching her when a shadow fell over me. Turning, I saw Braden standing in front of me.

"You were going to give me a tour of the house." He held out his hand to me. I took it and let him pull me to my feet.

"Let me show you my abode." I kept hold of his hand and led him into the house.

Chapter 17

Braden

Holding Ryan's hand could very quickly become my favorite thing to do.

We walked into the kitchen amidst the chaos of the breakdown of the party. Her Aunts were gathering belongings and sending off families. It was wonderful to see so much joy and happiness in a family. I'm not blind to the fact that there can be squabbles and contention in all families. But on that day, everything seemed to be right with their world.

The basketball game had been eye-opening. I remembered playing pick-up games in high school with some of those guys. What I did not remember was that basketball was a full-contact sport. There was everything except full-on tackling. The game ended because one of the guys got a bloody nose, and no one wanted to play while he had tissue hanging from his nose. Even in full-assault basketball, there are some standards. I took my share of hits. There would be a few bruises and some soreness tomorrow.

I noticed Ryan watching at some point, and after that, I tried to play better. I'm not saying I didn't get in a few good hits. I was trying to look good for her. What I did do was not whine as much as some of the others.

"Babe! Did you see what that guy did? You gonna help me out here?" That particular remark was met with derision from all the wives watching. Not to mention the lone sister of the player he was complaining about, who offered to clean his clock for his next game.

There was a round of ribbing. One of the guys approached the whining guy and told him he did not want that. She was known for her pointy elbows. Everyone laughed except the guy whining. He just looked scared. Ryan's family was crazy.

As we walked by the wall phone, it rang, making me jump. Someone close to it answered. I felt Ryan move toward them before I saw her.

"Hello. Yes, this is Ryan's house. Yes. I think Annie is still here. Who is this? I'll go see if I can find her."

Annie grabbed the woman who answered by the arm. Whispering, "Who is it?"

"They said it's your mom," They whispered as well, though they looked confused by her not taking the phone.

"Crap, did you say I was here for sure?"

"No, I said I had to go look. I didn't see you."

Ryan grabbed the phone off the counter. "Hi, this is Ryan. Annie left a few minutes ago. No, I don't know if she was heading back to her place. If I see her, I will tell her you called looking for her. Is there anything I can help with?"

Annie was making stop motions with her hands. Ryan turned away from her.

"No, ma'am. I guess I couldn't help with that. Goodbye." Ryan hung up the receiver and turned to Annie. "Your mom called. And she is trying to find you. You have not checked in with her about the party she's organizing. I am to tell you that you need to call her soon.

"Thanks, I'd better head out so you aren't telling too much of a lie."

I watched as Annie left the house. Everyone had quieted down when Ryan picked up the phone. As Annie left, they started talking again.

"I'm going to show Braden around. If you leave before I come back to the kitchen, it was nice seeing you." Taking my arm, she led me to the living room.

Like the other rooms downstairs, tables had been set up earlier. Now that they had been taken down, I could see how empty the place was.

"Planning to do some decorating, or are you a minimalist?"

"Neither. I've been slowly getting what I need. Believe me, everyone wants to give me furniture that is taking up space in their house." She slowly looked around the room. "I want what I put in here to have meaning to me."

"Sounds like a good plan." I looked around at the walls. There was some art on the walls. Not much, but a few pieces. Lots of empty wall space.

Ryan looked around at the walls as well. "I find art at local showings or at art fairs. Sometimes the art department at the high school has a showing of the students' art. Once in a while. They sell some pieces. I got that one there." She pointed at a large painting hanging between windows.

It was a beautiful close-up of a sunflower. The artist had captured all the seeds, and amongst the petals there was a small bee. I turned to look at her when I noticed the bee.

"Do you have an affinity for bees?"

"No," she laughed. "That only happened to me once before. And that was a long time ago. You never forget the feeling, though.

"I bet."

She took me by the hand and led me to a hallway. "This goes to what was my grandmother's room, which is now my study, and the downstairs bathroom. I kept as many of the pictures as I could. A lot of them are of my mom and her siblings. Some of them are of Jared, Jason, and me. The ones that I wasn't in or that didn't have my mom, I let others take when she died. I should say Rose let others take. As the older daughter, she had a say in where things went. My Uncle Jake didn't want to say anything. He said he already had the greatest treasure."

"Meaning you?"

"I think so. My grandmother died the year before I graduated from college. I would stay here when I came back on breaks sometimes. I asked Annie if she wanted to live here and be roommates, but she wanted her own space." She paused, looking around. "We were roommates in college. What about you? What was growing up like for you?"

"It was a fairly typical life, I guess." I continued down the hall, looking at the pictures. "There was so much happiness in your family.

"Pictures are great for showing the good times. There was a lot of pain as well. Most people don't put up pictures of their worst moments as a family. Everyone wants to be reminded of the good times. Even pictures that were taken at my grandmother's funeral, like this one." Ryan moved down the hall and pointed at a picture of a group of people piled together for a photo. Everyone was smiling and hugging each other. "If I didn't tell you that the photo was taken at a funeral, would you know?"

I looked closely at the picture. If Ryan hadn't told me about the reason everyone was gathered together, I would have thought it was a happy family gathering. And not a sad occasion. "Why did everyone look so happy?"

Ryan reached out to the photo and touched some of the faces. "We were happy to be together. I hadn't seen some of these people in a while. Everyone was off at college or starting their lives. I rarely see Rose's children anymore. They live in other places. Rose goes on what she calls a pilgrimage. Travels to see them at their various places. No one ever comes back to the nest."

She walked into the room at the end of the hall. I glanced into the bathroom. I am by nature a nosy person. I noticed the pink tiles and the little poodles. I didn't realize that Ryan had come back until she said something.

"Those pink tiles are the originals. Not sure how they survived the wildness of our family. My grandmother loved the retro feel of this bathroom. The pink makes me a little crazy sometimes. I don't think I could change it, though. It reminds me too much of her." She took my hand and pulled me to the room at the end of the hall.

Where the rest of the house didn't feel lived in, this room was the heart and soul of the place. The walls were covered with shelves. If there wasn't a window, it was a shelf. Each shelf was covered with books, some stacked on their sides so she could fit more on the shelf. I started looking at the book titles.

"Is there a system to this?" I motioned around the room to the various shelves. Some of the books I looked at were fiction, but the books next to them were nonfiction. There were books on meditation next to books on running.

"Of course, there is a system to this. Otherwise, I would never find them. This is a shelf of all the books I loved and sometimes reread." She motioned to the other shelves in order around the room. "These are mysteries, fantasy, fairytales, self-help, etc."

I looked closely at the titles on the shelves. "There is a book about politics on the fantasy shelf."

"What can I say, I shelve them as I see them."

I turned my attention to the rest of the room. A beautiful table covered in tiles was being used as a desk. "Did you do this?"

"What, the tile work?" I nodded as I ran my hand over some of the tiles. They were beautiful. "Annie and I did that. We found the table in a free pile by the side of the road. It was generally in good shape, but the top was scarred and gouged. We saw a video of someone who had restored a table using tiles, so we looked into it. I ordered the tiles from a place that hand-paints them. We bought them slowly and steadily until we had enough for the top. My uncle Jake helped us."

I looked at the chair conveniently placed by the large windows. It had a crocheted blanket on the back and a large puffy ottoman. I sat down in the chair and instantly felt comfortable. There was no need to adjust myself until I felt like I was in the right position.

"That is the best chair ever. It was my grandmother's chair." She sat down in the other comfortable chair in the room. "You very carefully avoided my questions about your own family."

"I'm good at that. There isn't much to say. My mom was a single mom. My Grandparents, her parents, live a few hours away. She grew up here for most of her childhood. The rest of the time was spent where my grandparents live now. After she had me, she moved back here. We lived with my father's parents for a while. My parents had known each other when she lived here and then met again in college. They both went to the state university. My mother taught at the elementary school while I was growing up. She still does. It's where I got my dream to be a teacher."

"What about your dad? You said you lived with his parents. Was he not part of your life?"

I felt around in my chest for the usual discomfort that I'd get when I was asked to explain about my father. It wasn't there. Ryan wasn't asking for any reason other than to find out about me as a person. There wasn't any morbid curiosity involved in her question, like there was with so many other people.

"My father died before I was born. He joined the military right before they were married. It had been his plan all along. To join up. He died in an accident a few months before I was born. She said the months before he died were very special. He would read to me while she was pregnant and talk to me all the time." Telling her about this, maybe because she had been so honest before about her past, was more poignant. "My mother moved in with her in-laws and stayed there after I was born. I was their only connection to their son, and she wanted me to have them in my life.

"Your mom is pretty strong."

"She is. After my grandparents died, she stayed in the house. She still lives there. I grew up on Potter Road. The one that runs behind the schools. I used to jump the fence, so I didn't have to walk around the block to enter the school. It used to drive my mother crazy. Not that she walked all the way around. She would go in at the gate by the high school. It was only a little farther down the road, but as a kid, that little bit was like a challenge. I would race her to see who could get to the school first."

"That sounds great. I don't think I had her as a teacher. How did I miss that?"

"She teaches third grade. The year we were in third grade, my mom took a sabbatical. She went back to college for a year and finished her master's degree. That way, she wouldn't have to deal with me as a student. Living with my grandparents made that type of thing possible. There was someone to take care of me when she wasn't home. It also meant that I didn't have to wait around the school like some of the other kids who had parents as teachers. It was a good childhood."

"How did we not know each other in school? It's not like this is such a huge town that we wouldn't have run into each other."

"You said yourself that you didn't socialize as a child. We probably saw each other but didn't connect. There were a lot of kids in the school, and there was more than one class per grade."

"You're probably right. I was pretty antisocial. I still am. I only talk to people at the library and try to avoid conversation otherwise."

"So, I'm the exception to the rule? You talk to me."

"If you remember, you cornered me at the library and then called my house. You were inescapable."

She smiled at me. It was one of those smiles that melted my heart with the sincerity she put behind it. The world was missing out on a wonderfully shy person. And I was so glad that they had. Because I was not going to blow this chance that I had with her.

"Oh, wow." She looked at something over my head. I looked to see a rather large cat with a clock in its stomach. If I saw it anywhere except on her bookshelf, I would have thought it was tacky. But it seemed to fit right in with the rest of the strange things tucked into the books. When I looked closer, I noticed a small bookshop that was lit up tucked into the shelves. I stood to look at it.

"Is that a book shop?"

"What, oh yeah. I put that together from a kit." She motioned at the clock again. "I didn't realize it was so late. We both have to work tomorrow."

Taking the hint, I made my way to the door. Her hand felt so right in mine.

She walked me to my car. I should have said goodbye at the door, but I couldn't make myself let go of her hand. I knew I would wait till she got back into the house before I left, but I just needed the extra few minutes.

"Thanks for inviting me. It was fun meeting your family. They are..." I paused, trying to figure out the right words.

"Strange, loud, bossy, opinionated, competitive. Take your pick."

"I was going to say loving. But those other words work as well."

She laughed at my response. I leaned back against the car, pulling her into a hug. I felt her sigh as she leaned into me. This felt right, too. All of this felt right.

Chapter 18

Ryan

Oh my, this felt like heaven. How had I somehow managed to make it to twenty-six without having been hugged like this? I have been hugged before, don't get me wrong. But this, this was amazing. I felt safe, warm, and content. I felt cherished. I've dreamed of being held like this.

Then he pulled back. Which I didn't think was possible, considering he was leaning against the car. He looked at me for a long minute. It was probably only a few seconds, but it felt like a long time, because I was now lost in his eyes. Either I have been reading too many romances, which I will admit could be the problem, or he was going to kiss me.

Did I want him to kiss me? Did I want that? I will go to my grave admitting that it was all I wanted at that particular moment in time. Except, he wasn't moving. Did I read this wrong? I'm not sure what I wanted to do. If I lifted a little and leaned, would he kiss me or pull away? Ugh, I hated this indecision. Maybe I should end the hug and go back in. I know that all these thoughts were going through my mind at the speed of light, because he hadn't moved.

What the heck, I was going to risk it. I stood up on my tiptoes a little and went for it. I pressed my lips to his. For a moment, nothing happened. Then he was kissing me back.

It has been described in books as though the world moved under the feet of the one being kissed. I don't know about that. I was too busy trying to ride out the cyclone of emotion that was raging through me. One simple kiss and I was forever gone.

His lips were soft as they moved gently over mine. No insistence. Only a slight pressure, a light touching of lips. He pulled back and pressed his forehead to mine. Our lips were so close, still only a slight movement away. I didn't want it to end. But as first kisses go, it was pretty amazing.

"I should probably head home now," he whispered. He gently moved his lips over my cheekbone. Then back to my lips for a gentle kiss.

When his lips went to the other cheek, I said, "Probably."

I didn't want this to stop. I leaned up and pressed my lips to his. And then I moved my mouth slowly, kissing his cheeks and then his lips again. Gently exploring his face.

Placing his hands on my shoulders, he pushed me back from him. Putting the necessary space between us.

"I think I should go."

"That would probably be best."

I stepped back from him and waited for him to get in the car. He opened the door and stood there.

"I'm not leaving until you're back in the house."

"Okay." I leaned in and kissed his cheek quickly before I ran up the steps to the door. I stood in the open doorway and watched him get in the car and start the engine. I waved as he started to pull out. Knowing he would wait at the end of the driveway for me to go in, I stepped back and closed the door. I was watching through the window as he drove off.

There was no way I was going to go to sleep anytime soon. I went down the hall to my study and plopped into the chair Braden had just been sitting in. It felt warm from his body. I reached behind me for the afghan I had made in college.

The semester I made the blanket had been a strange one. I had tried going out with a few guys. They asked, and I said yes, then the awkwardness ensued. So much awkwardness. It was after my third date that the rumors started going around. I'm not sure if they were rumors or public safety announcements about my level of anxiety and awkwardness. I can not express the depths of humiliation I felt when I accidentally pushed my date off the bridge we were walking on. I don't even think I can describe what happened. One minute he was standing there, and the next he was in the water. Thank goodness he was on the college swim team. In any case, that was my last date in college.

After that, I spent my Friday nights, well, every night, crocheting a blanket. I think I made around ten that semester. It was all I did: eat, go to class, do homework, sleep, and crochet. Everyone was thankful for their Christmas presents, if not a little confused by the sheer number of blankets.

The word spread, and no one asked me out. Annie was the one to tell me about it. Her date had asked her if she feared for her life as my roommate. I'm not sure if he meant it in a funny way or seriously. It was the last date he went on with Annie.

I wish I could say that I took it all in stride and wasn't bothered by it. But I was. I mean, who wouldn't be bothered by it? Luckily, it was our last year, and I didn't have to endure more time there. When we got back home after graduation, I offered Annie a room. But she stayed with her mom for a few weeks after we got our jobs at the library. Then she moved into a place of her own. A small apartment, more like a studio, over Mabel's garage.

I was worried that Mabel would keep too close an eye on Annie, but she said it was fine. She never saw Mabel except at the library. It would have been nice to have a roommate. It was also nice to have my own space for the first time. I wished there was someone I could talk to about what had just happened. It was also good to hold that memory for my own.

I snuggled deeper into the chair. Sometimes, the comfort level of the chair inhibited my reading. I had fallen asleep there more times than I could count. I listened to the sound of the clock quietly ticking on the shelf behind me.

I reached for my phone, pulling it out of my pocket. I pulled up the music app and played the soft music I listened to when I read. It was soft jazz that relaxed my body. The last thing I remembered was thinking that the music had maybe been a bad idea.

Chapter 19

Ryan

I woke up late. I barely had time to get a shower and grab my things. I had checked the weather and decided I would take advantage of the beautiful Spring day and ride my motorcycle to the library.

When I pulled in, I noticed Kate sitting in her car. Either she had just gotten there, or she was hiding from something.

I waited till she saw me, then waved. She waved back. She watched me watch her. With a sigh, she gathered up her things and got out of the car.

"Were you hiding in your car?"

"No, I was not hiding." I looked her in the eye and waited. It was a trick Janet had used with us growing up. She would stand there without saying anything and stare into our eyes. "Fine, I was hiding. It gets lonely in there during the day. I am not very well known here yet, and people don't seem to need to stop by for anything. I write my sermon on Monday, then I sit around staring at the walls. I was thinking of taking up watching Korean soap operas. Luckily, the secretary is only part-time. Or else she would have been telling the rest of the hiring committee that I didn't have anything to do."

We both leaned back against her car and watched the traffic go by on the road. You could see quite a lot if you looked up the driveway between the two buildings.

"My aunts said that there are a few openings in the book club. They are trying to bring in new blood. Preferably, people who actually read the book, since they have enough of the ones who don't. "

"What type of books do they read?"

"It varies. They are currently reading mysteries. There was a small window of time when they read non-fiction. No one could decide what type of non-fiction. One month, they all chose a cookbook to read and then made something to share at the next meeting. I think that was one of my favorites. Probably because Annie and I got to taste the food."

"That sounds fun."

"Be warned. The meetings can sometimes get loud and rowdy. How are your conflict resolution skills?"

"Pretty good. I make sure that I am up to date on all my trainings."

I laughed. "You'll do. Text Janet and ask when the next meeting is. The meetings are rarely at the same time. They do meet once a week. It will be the perfect opportunity for you to meet people and hear all the gossip about your parishioners. Never the slanderous kind. Usually, "what is happening in everyone's life" kind of gossip. Who had a baby, and who needs help with something, type of gossip.

"Thanks. I will. This might just save me from watching the K-dramas."

"The book club has plenty of drama for you."

I wandered off towards the library as Kate headed into the church. It was a good start to my morning. I hoped.

The confusion that began the day should have been a sign. Frank had forgotten that Annie had taken the day off. It took him a few minutes to find the schedule and see that, yes, she was off.

"Why would she do that? I just got back from vacation."

"Maybe that was why she did that," I mumbled as I went to empty the overnight returns. Some days there were only a few books; other days, like this one, I needed the wagon to bring them all in.

I had just finished checking the books back in when Tammy showed up. I told Frank I needed to take books to the Children's room. Mabel was working today. I scurried off before Tammy got close to the desk.

"Hi, I have all your returns."

"I would have come up for them." Mabel came out from behind her desk and started to sort the books off the cart.

"I know; I needed a minute away from the desk."

"Did Tammy come in?"

"How did you guess?" I helped her transfer the books to her cart. When I put them on the cart to transport, I always tried to separate them into their shelves. "I told Kate about the book club. Janet said you're looking for new members."

"Did she?"

That two-word sentence had an ominous feel to it. Once again, I had fallen into some nefarious plot in the book club. The last one was about a bake sale. Mabel wanted the club to do a bake sale to raise money for children's programs over the summer. There was a temporary replacement in charge because Frank was out due to emergency surgery. We were never told the exact nature of the surgery, and we did not want to know. Margie said everything was going well, and honestly, that was all we wanted. We knew that when Frank got back, he would regale everyone with the details, whether they wanted to know or not.

The new librarian had some issues with children and libraries. Crazy, I know, but there are some people out there who still believe that libraries should be as silent as the tomb. People should use their indoor voices, but I have never told anyone to shush. Except one time, and that was completely called for. It was a promposal, and the guy in question decided singing a Taylor Swift song at full volume in an enclosed space was a good idea. He also had a karaoke machine. Need I say more?

Back to the bake sale. The proposed bake sale was cancelled by the temp, and all chaos ensued. The bake sale was rescheduled and held at the church next door. Just off the library property. With a sign that said something along the lines of save our children. The sign alone brought in the buyers. Needless to say, the summer program was fully funded, and I replaced the temp until Frank came back. It was the first time I was left in charge. It was terrifying.

Though that plot was hatched against an outside force, the book club has had its internal strife. I didn't want to be included in it. And yet, somehow, my aunts had put me right in the middle.

"Even if she hadn't said anything, I would have suggested it. The woman needs some help and friendship. Who better than all of you lovely women?"

"Are you trying to butter me up?"

"Yes, I really am. I like living."

Mabel started laughing, which made me feel a little better about my chances of surviving.

"I'll go talk to her when I take my lunch break." She put the last book on the shelf, which was my signal to leave. I looked at the clock; Tammy should be gone by now.

"I also told her that the book club was who she should talk to about her plans to revitalize the congregation."

"You know there is a church board, right? That helps with that stuff," Mabel said.

"How many of the book club are on that board?"

"Go away and get back to work."

I went up the stairs slowly, trying to listen for Tammy's voice. I was just peering around the corner when a dinosaur jumped in front of me.

"ROAR!"

I am not proud, and I'll admit that I screamed and practically fell back down the stairs.

"Oh, Ryan. Are you okay?" Esther came to help me up.

"Yup. I'm fine. Just took me by surprise."

I looked over at the little dinosaur. He was close to tears. I think I scared him with my scream more than he scared me.

"That was some intense roar you got there. What type of dinosaur are you today?" He was the same as he always was—a very small T. Rex. "Are you heading downstairs?"

"Yes." Great, I had scared him down to one-word answers.

"I know for a fact that there are three new dinosaur books down there. I just put them on the shelf."

I was almost knocked over again, only this time in his rush to get down the stairs.

"You sure you're okay?" Esther asked on her way down the stairs. I only had time for a wave before she was gone.

When I came out into the library, Frank was staring at me. "What?"

"Was that you screaming? I thought someone was playing a horror movie over there."

"Funny, Frank. Isn't it time for you to go to lunch?" He always went to lunch first. Which meant that he had a very early lunch. With Annie gone, I would be alone on the floor. There were a few other librarians here. I would call one of them and ask for help if I needed it.

"Yes, do you want me to pick anything up when I am out?"

"No, I have leftovers from the cookout last night."

"You had a cookout, and we weren't invited? I bet Annie was there. And most of the book club." He started to sulk his way back to his office.

"Annie is my best friend, and I'm related to half the book club."

"Whatever," he mumbled.

When he left for lunch, I settled into my desk after checking to see who was in the library. Most of the patrons were downstairs.

It was barely lunch, and my nerves were shot.

When my lunch break came, I headed out the door. I told Frank I would be gone for the whole hour and that he needed to hold down the fort. The look on his face was priceless. He loved not having to work the desk anymore. He had found his paradise, and it was the little office.

I wandered over to the church. Something Kate had said when we were talking had hit a nerve with me. We were talking about Tammy and something she had done while we were at the coffee shop that first day, Katherine mentioned working with bullying victims in her last congregation.

I went in through the open door in the back. The one that led to the offices. I saw her secretary, Patty, as I rounded the corner.

"Hi, is Kate free at the moment?"

"I don't know, I'll have to check."

She was just picking up the phone when Kate opened the door. "Hello, I thought I heard your voice." She looked over at Patty, "I'm going to chat with Ryan. Is there anything happening in the next hour?"

"Nope, you're clear. I'm heading off to lunch."

"Enjoy your lunch." She motioned me into the room.

"Sorry to make you miss your lunch."

"I have been so unbusy this morning that I have been stress eating the baked goods I brought with me from Connie's. What's up?"

"You heard a little about Tammy the other morning."

"I did."

"She has been the bane of my existence for most of my life. Well, basically, since middle school, except when I went to college. I saw a therapist for a while after my mother died and then again when I was in college."

"Very wise."

I smiled. "It felt more like a necessity. Anyways, it isn't that she is ever overtly attacking me, it is just the little things that wear me down. It is almost like a Pavlovian experience. I see her, and I begin to panic. She doesn't even have to say anything. She only needs to be in the room. What I'm trying to say is I can't keep doing this. I know I have social anxiety; large crowds and new places can trigger me. The type

I feel with her is so much more like needing to defend myself from a physical attack."

"You probably feel that way because you *are* under attack. She is attacking you. So, feeling that way is natural. The fact that it is not a physical attack doesn't change the fact that it is an attack. The thing is, your response feeds that attack. Does she say things to anyone else? Annie, for instance?"

"She does. Annie looks at her and says nothing. It's like what she says hits an impenetrable wall and dies."

"Have you tried that?"

"Tried what?"

"Not reacting, just ignoring her." Kate leaned back in her chair, looking at me. "I am going to tell you a story. When I was in school, there was someone who bullied me, just as Tammy bullies you. She would wear me down with her little quips. All meant to make me feel small. I would try to take up less space, giving her more space. Not that this in any way excuses her for her behavior, more of an explanation, she was jealous of something about me. Whether it was that I was smarter, there was some guy she liked, whatever it was, she felt threatened. And her way of dealing with it was to assert her importance. When I stopped listening to her, I started to feel less intimidated and less afraid."

"How did you do that?"

"This is weird; I picked a song that pumped me up when I listened to it. In my case, it was a Spice Girls song. Every time I saw her, I would start singing it in my head. It got to the point where I didn't hear her whispers because I was concentrating on the song. I even saw her once and started to sing in my head, and I danced a little. That was moderately embarrassing for other reasons. Once, when she was next to me, I started to sing it quietly under my breath. That threw her off completely. She realized I wasn't listening to her. She ceased to be important, and I think she saw my responses to her comments kind of like how Tammy sees Annie's response. Like it is hitting against a wall."

"You actually started to sing while she was talking to you?"

"I did."

We both started to laugh—me at the absurdity of how that must have looked and her at the memory.

"Did she stop?"

"To be honest, I don't know. I just stopped listening. I think that's the trick: to stop listening. To stop letting her be so important in your life."

We talked about other stuff for the rest of the time I was there. On my way out, I asked her about singing the song out loud.

"I turned to her to ask her what she wanted. Only it came out as the song, and I was asking her to tell me what she really wanted. I don't know who was more surprised, her or me. "

"It is definitely food for thought," I said.

I had so much to think about. The morning conversations, the kiss, and now this. Was there a song that I could sing to drown her out? My options were many.

Chapter 20

Braden

I spent the ride to work in the morning thinking of that kiss. Where did that kiss come from? I was trying to take things slow. Give us time to get to know each other again. I guess that was what we had been doing with all those hours-long phone calls—getting to know each other.

We talked about everything. It feels easier to tell someone your life story while you're looking at your comfortable surroundings. You can't see their face and see their reactions. Some reactions show up before you can stop them from appearing on your face. With phone calls, there's a sense of safety. I told her about my life, what I have done, my dreams about the future, and my fears from the past more than anyone else. I guess we have gotten to know each other. Huh, I hadn't realized how much I knew about her.

I was early to school. We had planned to meet before school to talk about the "multi-disciplinary" project. Whether or not we ever got the project up in the air was irrelevant. It was fun to think about and an excuse to meet, have coffee, and talk about our lives.

Brian was never big on talking; he was big on watching Lydia talk. He had better ask Lydia out soon, or Stan and I are going to set them up on a blind date with each other so they don't escape. That was actually a great idea. I'll have to talk to Stan.

Slipping past Mrs. Tussle was getting harder every day. She had rearranged her office to see the hallway regardless of what she was doing. Sneaking past her was becoming an art form. I looked around the hallway for an idea of how to get past the door. Fate provided the answer in the form of a media cart moving my way. I couldn't see who was pushing the cart. Which meant that it was Jackie from the math department. She was short enough that she had to look around the cart instead of over. Usually, she had a student bring the cart to the class. Today, thankfully, she was pushing it herself, and I had the distraction I needed.

I moved back to the end of the hall and walked alongside the cart. Quietly talking to her as we walked. As it got closer to the door, I stooped down until I was below the level of the cart. Smiling and shaking her head at me, we moved past.

"Morning, Mrs. Tussle, no time to stop." She kept walking. I heard a faint, "Good morning," as we made it past.

"You owe me, Braden," Jackie said as she made the corner.

I waved as I kept going down the hall. I would need to bring her a coffee or a muffin. Her distracting Tussle was going above and beyond. For some reason, she was one of Mrs. Tussle's favorites. She, like me, graduated from this high school. I remembered her a grade ahead of me. Always polite, always friendly. It was hard not to like her.

I would ask Lydia what the story was with her. It's always good to know about those you work with, especially if you ever need to ask for a favor, like covering lunch for you.

I saw Stan leaning against my door. "Hey, Stan. How are you?"

"How am I? I am stilling recover from the stress of getting here. I barely made it past Tussle. How did you get past her?"

We entered the room and set up some chairs around a side table. I even moved the portable whiteboard closer, all to make this seem more realistic. One of these days, we might have to give a report on our findings. We said we were in the process of working everything out every time Tussle asked. At some point, she was going to call our bluff.

"I used a diversionary tactic. I hid behind the media cart Jackie was pushing. I now owe her a muffin."

"Jackie's here early?"

Stan was looking thoughtfully out the door. Had I missed something at the staff meetings? Was there love blooming?

"Yup, and pushing that cart down the hall. She said hello, sidetracking Tussle from seeing me."

"That was nice of her."

"Have you asked her out yet?"

"What," Stan gasped. "Ask her out? What are you, crazy?" He started to pull out the coffee he had brought with him. He paused in placing the cups on the table. "Do you think she'd go out with me?"

"I don't know. You could always ask her."

"I think she's going out with someone."

"We'll ask Lydia. She knows all this stuff. Speaking of Lydia. We need to do something about those two. I was thinking about a blind date. I can set Brian up; you set Lydia up."

"Do you think that would work?'

I looked at him while I thought, "I don't know. Maybe. It would be worth a try, wouldn't it?"

We both turned to see Lydia and Brian come into the room. Lydia was talking, and Brian was walking just behind her with a look of—I wasn't sure what that look was. It was more than the way a friend looked at another friend; I knew that.

"Ready to begin our discussion?" Lydia sat down and lifted the lid on her cup."Oh, my favorite. Thanks, Stan."

"No problem."

I waited until everyone was seated before I went to close the door. Looking down the hall before I fully closed it, I saw Jackie hurry toward me. She was waving.

"Hi, what's up?"

"Can I join you this morning?" She motioned to the cup in her hand. "I brought my own. I always wanted to be part of your group.

Please?" How could I say no to someone who batted their eyelashes at me and gave me a pouty face?

"Sure," I said as I gave one last glance before finally shutting the door.

"Hello, everyone," Jackie said as she crossed the room.

"Welcome. Finally, another woman. I won't be so outnumbered." Lydia moved her chair over, making room for Jackie.

"I always wondered what you did in these secret meetings. Sometimes, if I'm honest, I've come down here and heard you all laughing. I saw you all sneaking in this morning and thought I would see if I could join the club."

"Are we that obvious," I asked.

"No, not really. I've been looking for somewhere to fit in at the school, so I thought I would see if I fit with you."

"I'm glad you did." Stan was trying to seem unexcited by this new development, but was failing miserably. Lydia turned towards me so those two couldn't see her and winked.

"Braden, how was the party at Ryan's last night? I hear you held your own in the basketball game. That can be tough with those guys."

"Jackie, how did you know I was there?"

"My sister is married to one of Rose's sons. She told me you were there and wanted me to tell her what I knew of you. You made a good impression. However, those cousins are all protective of Ryan and will want to check you out to make sure you're good enough."

"I didn't know you were going to Ryan's house last night. How come you didn't tell us?" Lydia was giving me the evil eye. She always did when she thought I was holding out information.

"I was going to tell you this morning."

"Sorry," Jackie whispered.

"No problem. Now, I don't have to come up with a way to start the conversation."

I told them about the last-minute invitation and meeting Ryan's family. Since Jackie knew a lot of them already, she didn't need any clarification and helped with putting people in the right families. They all laughed at the basketball stories, though Brian didn't believe they were that cutthroat until Jackie told a few stories her sister had told her of games in the past.

We realized it was time to go to our classrooms when the students started trickling in. We made plans for our next morning meeting before everyone left. Brian was the one who mentioned some sort of idea for our interdisciplinary project. He thought some sort of scavenger hunt through the departments where there were clues connecting various points in math, history, and literature. It was the first idea anyone had come up with, a good talking point if we were ever cornered about our meetings and any progress we had made.

As the student trickled in, I realized I was really looking forward to the end of the school day. I had finally come up with an idea for a date night with Ryan. And with the help of our new friend Jackie, I knew just where to take her.

At the end of the day, I made my way to the library. I had two purposes for the visit: to ask Ryan out and to find a book to read. I had finished the last one Ryan had recommended and needed a new one.

I was coming through the doors when I heard Tammy's voice. Her voice was beginning to bug me. It had started to take on the tone of fingernails on a chalkboard. I would hear it, and instantly, my hackles would go up. It set off a very protective streak I didn't know I had. I was in the process of following it when I saw Ryan. She was shelving books while Tammy walked along beside her. Asking her annoying questions. That, if taken at face value, they were just as innocuous as Ryan had said. But the questions suddenly became very offensive when you heard Tammy's tone. I stopped to watch what was happening, ready to move in and interrupt if needed.

"Tammy, excuse me. I need to put this there." Ryan gently moved Tammy back so she could put the book on the shelf. For all intents and purposes, Ryan was not hearing Tammy at all. I could see the look of shock on Tammy's face from a mile away.

"Can you hear me?"

"What, I'm sorry, I couldn't hear you. Did you say something?" Ryan reached up and took a small earbud from her ear. She had been listening to something on her earbuds the entire time Tammy talked.

"I can not believe you did that. You were ignoring me on purpose."

Ryan looked at her and then did something I never thought I would see. She smiled and said, "Of course I was. Was there a book you needed? Otherwise, I'm busy." She put the earbud in and walked off to the next shelf.

Tammy looked enraged. She glared at the back of Ryan's head before heading off toward the front desk. I could hear her complaining. Everyone could hear her complaining.

I moved up beside Ryan and put my hand on her arm. She jumped.

"I'm sorry. I didn't mean to scare you. Are you okay?"

"Is she gone?" Ryan looked around the area furtively. She slowly took the earbuds out of her ears. I took one from her to see what she was listening to. I didn't recognize the song, though it sounded familiar.

"She's up yelling at Frank," I said.

"That won't help her much. It was Frank's idea. I went and spoke to Kate about Tammy during my lunch break. She had some good ideas." Ryan went on to tell me all of the things they had spoken of, including the music as a distraction. "When I got back to the library, I spoke with Frank. I explained what Kate had said about the singing. It was then that Frank insisted that I wear my earbuds when she was in the building and direct her to other places."

I watched as she reached out to the shelf and held on. She started to breathe in through her nose slowly and then out through her mouth, something I had seen my mother do a time or two.

"Is there anything I can do?"

"No, I'm okay. What brings you to the library?

"You and the need for a book." She smiled at me and took my hand, leading me over to a couple of chairs tucked in by the window. She leaned in and kissed my cheek before we sat down.

"How can I help?"

"Will you go out to dinner with me tomorrow? I want to take you someplace nice."

"Yes, I would love to."

I felt myself relax. That was the hard part. I wasn't sure if she would go out with me. She had said that she didn't like to try new places.

"The next thing is I need a book. Any recommendations?"

"As a matter of fact, I do." She took my hand again, and we walked to the new-release shelf. "Do you read fantasy? Oh, right, you said that you did. This is new; I read good things about it, and the people who have checked it out seemed to like it."

I took the book and opened it, reading the inner flap. It did sound like something I'd like. She always seemed to know what books people would like. She had said in one of our long phone conversations that she paid attention, saw what people read most often, and went from there. It still seemed like a magic trick.

I walked with her to the counter, where she checked the book out for me. "I'll pick you up at your house. Would seven be good?"

"Seven would be great. I'm looking forward to it." She still seemed off from her encounter with Tammy. But I let it go. I figured that if there were a problem, Annie would know how to help her better than I could. She didn't seem to want to talk to me about it.

Chapter 21

Ryan

"I can't wear that!" Annie held out a dress to me that I would never, ever consider wearing.

"What? This would look great. You have good muscle tone. And it doesn't show very much of your leg. That one,"—she pointed at my choice—"is..."

"Is what? What is wrong with it? I like it. I know it's a little long. But I feel good when I wear it. It has a wild feel to it."

The dress in question was a beautiful rose color. It had layers and came to mid-calf. I liked how it floated around me. I also didn't feel as exposed as I would in the dress Annie was showing me. I needed something comfortable. Something that didn't feel constricting anywhere. The last thing I needed was to feel claustrophobic in my clothes. I was struggling with my anxiety enough as it was.

"It hides you."

"It doesn't hide me. I am not hiding. It shows off my curves in a nice way. Subtle. And you are not going to change my mind."

I stepped into the dress and pulled it up over my body. We had worked on the makeup earlier. Even though I liked the less-is-more vibe I usually had, Annie did my face for me, and it felt like she put a lot more on than I do. It was all secretive. The big reveal at the end of getting me ready.

"Sit here and don't move." Annie had brought one of the kitchen chairs into the bedroom.

"Why do we have to do this here? Everything for my hair is in the bathroom?" She ran the brush a little forcefully through my hair. "There are no mirrors in here, and you would peek. I know you."

It took far less time for her to do my hair than it would have taken me. My ability to reach behind my head and do a French braid was nonexistent. I would have just left it down or put it into a braid. Annie knew, and that was the main reason for coming to help me.

I would have worried the whole time that I was doing it wrong. I would have created more and more anxiety until I worked myself up to canceling before he could get to the house. This is why Annie followed me home and marched into my house behind me, refusing to leave.

"Okay, I think we are finished."

I went into the bathroom to look at myself in the mirror behind the door. I looked and then closed my eyes. When I opened them, I was still standing there, or at least someone who resembled me was standing there.

"Wow, I don't look like myself."

"What do you mean? You look exactly like yourself." She came up next to me and put her arm around my waist, pulling me into her side. We stood looking in the mirror for a few minutes. "Do you remember when we got ready for Prom at my house?"

"Yes. It was quite the ordeal. My aunts were both there."

"Thank goodness. They contained the comments from my mother. She was in rare form that night."

"We got ready at your house and then travelled back to my house to be picked up. Why did we do it that way again?"

"Because your cousins were getting ready at your house, and we needed more space."

"Right, getting ready in the same house as those two would have been a nightmare."

We were both still laughing about it when there was a knock at the door.

"You want me to get it?" Annie nudged me before she started to head to the door.

"No, I'll get it. That way, I can just leave. If I wait longer, I might panic."

"It's okay. You're going to have fun with Braden. You've had a good time the other times you were together."

"Yes, but those were familiar places. I don't want him to see me have a panic attack."

"You are going to be fine. Everything is going to be fine. And if it isn't, you know what to do."

"Run screaming from the room?" Annie didn't even respond. She gave me one of her glares instead.

"You can do this. I believe in you." Annie reached into a drawer and handed me a box. I had been keeping that box safe for a long time. "Wear these. And hurry up, he's waiting."

She went to open the door for Braden since I wasn't moving in any direction very fast. I held the box and felt all sorts of different emotions. Annie knew I was saving these for a special occasion. I guess this was a special enough occasion.

I opened the box and stared at my mother's earrings. I could hear Braden and Annie talking. I slowly reached up and took out the earrings I had put in only a few minutes before. As I put my mother's earrings in, I looked in the mirror at my reflection. I resembled my mother in many ways. With her earrings in, I could feel her with me. I had backup. I had Braden, and I had my mother. What could possibly go wrong?

APPARENTLY, EVERYTHING could go wrong. When we got to the restaurant, they had lost the reservation. Which was fine. It wasn't a busy night. The confusion involved in getting a table was difficult. I began to feel tingling in my fingers as Braden talked to the hostess. I looked around at the other diners to see if there was anyone I knew. The memories of other dates that had gone wrong replayed in my head.

If Annie were here, she would make fun of me, and I would laugh it off. But Annie wasn't here. Braden smiled at me and apologized. There was really nothing for anyone to apologize for. Stuff like that happens all the time. No one was inconvenienced. The Hostess led us to our table. Braden pulled out my chair for me and kissed my cheek before he went to sit down.

The problem with my anxiety is that I can get triggered when I am in a new place or when I am with people I don't know. My therapist and I would come up with strategies to get me through the first weeks of the semester when I went to college until things became familiar. After things became familiar, I usually didn't have any problems.

I had explained some of this to Braden on the way to the restaurant. He listened and then took my hand and said, "I've got you. Just tell me what you need."

Did I believe him? Yes, with all my heart. Did I think that I would be safe? Yes. Sort of.

"I don't know what I need."

"Okay, we can just play it by ear. If you need anything, let me know."

While I looked at the menu, Braden started talking to me. He talked about everyday things. Nothing specific. Everything in his quiet, soothing voice. The evil part of my brain that always tried to sabotage me was whispering about being broken. I shut that down as fast as I could.

I looked around the room again, noticing the people around us. That was a mistake. The more I looked around, the more my skin started to feel prickly. I could feel the uncontrolled need to run start to build.

At that moment, Braden reached across the table and put his hand on my arm. "Where are you?"

"Trying not to fly apart."

"Why, what's changed in the last few minutes?"

"I don't know."

"Eyes on me. I want to see your eyes. You look incredible tonight. Did I say that earlier? If not, I should have. You take my breath away."

I looked over at him. He really could rock a suit. "I should say the same. You look good tonight. I noticed your shirt was even tucked in."

That got a laugh out of him. "You caught me. There is something about a tucked shirt that makes me feel trapped. I have no idea where it came from, but it is something I have always struggled with. My mother could tell you stories about epic battles to get me to tuck my shirt in."

I laughed with him. I felt the need to fly apart start to recede. I was starting to relax. I was going to make it.

We talked for a few more minutes. The waiter took our drink orders. Mine was water, and his was some sort of lemonade that I hadn't heard of. Since neither of us drank alcohol, the drinks menu was small. The waiter was almost to our table when I heard the laugh.

It was familiar. And at the same time, it wasn't familiar. All the relaxation that had been surrounding me went away very quickly. I looked around the room to see who was laughing. Maybe I could recognize them. There was no one in the dining room that I knew or even vaguely knew.

"Are you okay?"

"I think so." I kept looking around. I couldn't see anything, and the laugh was gone. "I think so," I repeated.

The level of my anxiety made itself known in a small tremor in my hands. This wasn't good. The room started to feel warm. I felt my chest start to constrict and expand as though I were hyperventilating. Which, when I paid attention to myself, I noticed I was. I looked at Braden. His eyes were focused on me. I could see his mouth moving, but I couldn't register any sound.

I was sitting there breathing hard and trying to focus. I knew I needed to stop. I needed to at least seem normal. That was the only way I could get to safety. If no one saw me panic.

I noticed Braden was standing. He was taking my arm, helping me up from the table, and leading me out. I looked around and saw that others were now looking at me. Staring at me as I slowly imploded into myself.

I focused inward and tried to focus all my energy on calming my breathing. If I could get my breathing to slow down to become normal, then the rest of my body would follow. It would try to become normal.

At the car, I realized Braden was helping me into my seat. He reached around me and fastened the seat belt. My breathing was slowing. My hands weren't clamped as tightly together. I was becoming more aware of what was going on around me.

"I'm sorry," I whispered.

"For what? Are you okay?" he glanced at me quickly and then around at our surroundings.

"Can you take me home?" My voice was so quiet that I could barely hear it.

"Of course. Everything is going to be okay. You're safe."

"My head knows that."

"But not the rest of you?"

"Sometimes there is a definite lag between what I know and feel. This is that time."

I reached into my bag and pulled out my phone. I quickly texted Annie, *SOS, my house*, and put my phone away before seeing if she read it.

"How can I help?"

"I don't know." I sat quietly before I whispered, "I am so sorry I ruined the date."

"Don't worry about it."

"I do worry. I haven't had an attack like this in a long time. And never in public. All those people saw me. They saw me go from a moderately functional person into a," I paused, not knowing what word to associate with what I felt like people saw. "I know it was an anxiety attack. I know that people have them. I know that a lot of people have anxiety. I know this with my head. My heart remembers the teasing and the bullying. My heart remembers the fear and the need to be somewhere safe when things weren't safe." I took a deep breath before I finished. "My brain knows the way people look at me with a combination of pity and aversion. They see someone incapable of going to a restaurant without freaking out. And I feel shame. Right now, I feel so afraid of unseen things that I don't know how to calm myself. And so ashamed for not being able to face the world without losing control."

"You have nothing to be ashamed of." He reached over and pried my hands apart, taking one of them in his own. "How can I help you?"

"Just get me home. I'll be better there."

"Okay." He looked at me before starting the car. Sighing, he said, "I'm sorry."

"For what? You didn't freak out and ruin the date."

"You didn't ruin it either."

I just nodded, not saying anything. I couldn't say anything. All the shame in the world was currently residing in my heart, replacing the panic with sadness and loss. I felt a tear start to roll down my cheek. I couldn't look at him. I didn't want to see rejection.

Chapter 22

Ryan

As Braden pulled into my driveway, I saw Annie's car already parked next to the garage. I kept my gaze away from Braden. I couldn't stand the thought of the pity I might see there.

When he brought the car to a stop, I hurried to get my seat belt off so I could quickly escape from the car. He reached over and caught my hand as I released my seat belt. "Wait. Let me walk you in. I want to make sure you're okay."

"I'll be okay. Thank you for trying to take me somewhere nice. I'm sorry I ruined the evening."

"You have nothing to be sorry about. I know you'll be okay. I should have listened when you said you struggled with new places. I want to walk you in."

"No, I'll be okay."

"I don't think you should be alone."

"I'm not. Annie's here." I heard another car pull into the drive. My aunt Rose got out of the car and headed toward the house. She looked at me, but I shook my head. "See you later. I'll call you, okay?"

Braden watched my aunt go into the house. He seemed to accept my not wanting him to walk me in."Okay."

I got out of the car and hurried toward the house. I turned as I got inside the door to see if he had left yet. He was still in the drive, watching me. I waved and shut the door. I peeked through the curtain. He was still there. He must have seen me because he waved before pulling out and driving off.

I felt warm arms wrap around me and turn me. I leaned into my aunt, and for the first time in a long time, I cried.

I couldn't stop the shaking and the crying. Rose led me to the table. Annie was already waiting for us there.

"Janet will be here in a few minutes. She was in the middle of a meeting with Katherine about someone who needed help."

We heard Janet's car come to a stop outside. I knew it was her by the sound of the car door. Her door had a squeak when she opened it too fast. It surprised me to hear a second door slam shut. I didn't have a chance to even wonder who she had brought with her before the door was shoved open.

The thing about the kitchen door is that it has a spring on it. I was forever worried about not closing the door when I came in. After a few instances of thinking I had shut the door and later finding it open, I installed a spring on the door to ensure it shut behind me. The spring was tight on the best of days and tended to slam back on you if you opened it too roughly. I had gotten caught in the door a couple of times and knew the spring needed to be loosened, but I just never remembered to do it when I had a chance.

Janet slammed the door open in her rush to come in, and the door slammed back. She hadn't come in the house very far and was shoved back outside. I heard a muffled squak and another voice asking if she was okay. Rose went to the door, holding it open for Janet to come through.

Following behind Janet was Kate.

"I didn't know if it would be okay for me to be here, but I heard you were having trouble." Kate moved over to me and put her hand on my shoulder.

I couldn't take my eyes off Janet. She stood there with ice cream dripping down her shirt. The same ice cream she had been carrying when the door attacked her. Janet glared at the door while mumbling under her breath. She put the now flattened container in the sink and pulled at her shirt.

"I'm going to borrow one of your shirts. I'll be right back. Don't talk about anything till I get back." She practically ran out of the room and up the stairs. It was a good thing she knew where everything was.

As I watched her go, I felt a smile start to form on my mouth. Then a giggle tried to break free. By the time it had made its way to freedom, it had become a full laugh. I couldn't stop thinking about the look on Janet's face when Rose opened the door—that moment seemed to have broken the spell the anxiety had on me. I felt myself relax for the first time since I had walked into the restaurant.

"Okay, what happened? All I know is that I got an SOS and was told to meet here." Janet came back into the kitchen at a fast clip but stopped when she saw me laughing. "It was not that funny. That door is a menace. Your uncle said he would be here tomorrow to fix it." She sat down in the available chair with as much dignity as she could.

"We don't know yet. You said not to talk before you got here." Rose sat down much more gracefully than Janet. All while not taking her eyes off of me.

"I completely humiliated myself at the restaurant. We had to leave."

"That leaves a lot of room for interpretation," Annie said. "Exactly how did you humiliate yourself?"

I told them about the panic attack, how Braden had gotten me out of the restaurant and into the car, and the embarrassing ride home.

"Did he say anything to you on the ride home? Anything that might make you think you scared him off?" Kate had found my stash of ice cream in the freezer. While we were talking, she was busy getting out the emergency ice cream. The container my aunt brought was a write-off.

I ate a few bites of the ice cream before saying anything. "He said that everything would be okay and that I was safe. He also said I didn't ruin the date." I pushed the ice cream out of the way and put my head on the table. "If that isn't ruining a date, I don't know what is." It took them a minute to decipher my mumblings.

"He was right about one thing. Everything is going to be okay." Kate rubbed my back while I kept my head down.

"Then why do I feel so broken?"

"You aren't broken, sweetie." Rose rubbed my back while she talked. Her touch always soothed. "Your brain works differently. That's all. It isn't broken."

"It feels broken. The tiniest thing, and I feel like I am under attack from an entire Zombie apocalypse."

"Wow," Annie said. "That got dark fast."

"Well, that's what it feels like. Any second, someone is going to grab me and eat my brain. And the only way to stay safe is to run. But there is no real threat and nowhere to run to."

"If there is a zombie apocalypse, I am going with you. I bet you already thought out all the escape routes and what to do." Annie was laughing at me.

"I will have you know that I have a planned safe room in the library, and I also know the fastest way to safety from any of the places I usually frequent."

"I knew it," Annie said.

"This is important information. You and I are going to have to talk," Kate said.

"Katherine, you can pick my brain anytime."

"This is so specific. What made you think of the Zombies instead of, say, a fire or something?" Janet pushed her empty bowl to the center of the table.

"A zombie apocalypse pretty much covers every possible disaster scenario. Think about it."

They were all quiet for a few minutes, thinking about the possible things involved with emergencies and an uprising of the dead.

"Well, on that note, I think I'm going to go home. Kate, can I give you a ride back to your car?"

"Thanks, Janet. That would be great."

Everyone started to pack up and leave. Rose left with Janet and Kate. After they closed the door. I noticed Annie was still sitting at the table. She hadn't moved to leave.

"Do you want me to stay with you tonight? I know sometimes you have a hard time sleeping after a big attack."

"Would you? I have the guest bed made up."

She squeezed my hand. "Of course. Let me get my bag from the car."

As she left to go to her car, I remembered her saying once that she had her version of a go bag. It contained clothes for the night, toiletries, and work clothes for the next day. I had asked her about it when I saw it by her front door. Her reply was, "So I'm ready if you need me."

I felt an intense sense of shame when she said it, and I started to cry. It was the first time I had articulated how broken I felt, that people had to be ready to stay with me if I panicked.

"It is because I love you. You're my best friend. I would do anything for you. It's not because you are broken. It is because you are a rare and beautiful gift to my life."

She had never had to use the go bag before. I was glad that she had it with her. I'd be embarrassed in the morning. Tonight, I felt a lot safer with her there, and that was all that mattered.

Chapter 23

Braden

I sat in my car watching as Ryan walked up to her house. Fragile didn't even begin to describe her. I know that she said she'd had attacks in the past during those long conversations on the phone. This was my first time witnessing one. I had seen other people say that they were having anxiety about something, or withdrawing from whatever or wherever they were, because, as they later said, they felt an attack coming on. But I had never seen the terror in someone's eyes as they struggled with that level of internal threat.

I wanted to stay and help, help her feel peaceful again. I wanted to see her smile. When she waved to me through the window, I put the car in gear and started to back out of the drive.

I didn't want to go home. All I'd do at home was sit and worry about her. Trying to figure out how to help. I would probably open up the laptop and start googling whatever information I could find on anxiety. As I drove down the road, I made a decision. When I reached the intersection, I turned right and started for the one place I knew I could go for help.

The lights at the front of the house were off. As I rang the doorbell, I hoped I wouldn't get into trouble coming so late without calling first. When the door opened, and I was met with a look of concern rather than censure, I relaxed. I felt arms wrap around me and pull me into a hug before pulling me into the house. I knew I had made the right decision.

"Mom, I have a problem. Maybe you could help me."

"Let's go to the kitchen. I'll put water on for tea."

I started by telling her about Ryan. "Do you remember the girl with the motorcycle in high school?"

"The librarian? Of course, I remember her. I talk to her every so often when I go to the library. She always has good recommendations."

"That's the one. Ryan. I ran into her not long ago. She had pulled over because a bee got into her clothes."

My mother started laughing. "You're the one who pulled over to help? That story seems to get better with each telling. Is she the woman you went out with tonight?" She glanced at the clock. "It seems early for your date to be finished. Is everything okay?"

"That's the problem. When we got to the restaurant, she seemed a little uneasy. Once we were inside, she started to panic. I mean, really panic. I have never seen anyone have an anxiety attack before. It scared me." My mother raised an eyebrow at me. "Not because I was embarrassed. I know I would have been when I was younger and more prone to being an idiot. It scared me because I wanted to keep her safe, and at the same time, I didn't know what to do."

"What did you do?"

"I took her home." I got up and started to pace the kitchen, moving from counter to counter, looking for something to distract me from the feeling of unease that was percolating in my stomach. "On the way to her house, she said that she was sorry so many times. There wasn't anything to be sorry about. I tried telling her that. She was also embarrassed to have panicked like that. She texted someone while I was driving her home, and by the time we got to her house, there was a car there, and one of her aunts showed up just as we pulled in. I knew she was safe and that she wasn't going to be alone. I just, I don't know, I don't like leaving her like that."

I finally sat back down at the table. And just like all the times I felt confused and troubled as a child, I put my head down, feeling the wood under my forehead. Letting it ground me. I had seen Ryan do the same thing. Another thing we had in common.

"Of course, you feel like this. It is a horrible feeling to see someone you love go through an anxiety attack like that. It used to make your grandfather crazy when I would have them. Your father never had them. Living with his parents was great in so many ways. But, they weren't my parents. Your grandfather always seemed like he was distancing himself from me. When the truth was, he didn't know what to do. And when he didn't know what to do, he would shut down. My mother would sit and hold my hand. Sometimes the act of holding my hand helped to ground me. Feeling that out of control because there is a threat you can't see, knowing it doesn't exist, and yet having your body act as though it is about to be hit by a car or chased by a predator, is terrifying. They were far away. All I had was my in-laws."

"I didn't know you had anxiety attacks."

"I do, though not like I used to. When you were little, everything felt so out of control. I felt so alone raising you. I was trying to do the right things for you. I was always worried. And that led to anxiety attacks." She stroked my hair as I kept my face down on the table.

"What did you do?"

"I met with someone. It helped me to talk about what was going on in my life. We came up with some strategies. The strategies helped me navigate the attacks when they came. I don't have them nearly as often anymore.

"What can I do to help her?"

"Ask her. Find out what she does. I'm sure she has some strategies for coping with them or mitigating the attacks when they do happen. It sounds like she tried to do something a little too hard and a little too quickly."

"She did say that she struggled going to new places. I thought if I were with her, it would be safe."

"Maybe she thought that, too. But the newness and being surrounded by people she doesn't know were probably just too much."

We sat quietly for a few minutes while I thought about what she had said. It was really presumptuous of me to think that my being there would mitigate all the things she worried about. "What should I do? How can I help her to know that I still want to see her?"

"Call her. Maybe not tonight. But don't let too much time go by before you talk to her. Don't put it off. Don't let her think she scared you away, unless she did scare you away?"

"She didn't scare me away." The more I talked, the more I realized that no, it didn't scare me away, and that I was in it for the long haul. Until I said those words to my mother, I hadn't realized that my feelings for her had become that important. I realized that I was falling in love with this woman.

She was everything I was looking for. She filled in all the empty places. I had dated before. And there always seemed to be a place in my heart that stayed closed off. But, Ryan, she opened all the doors in my heart and made me feel things I didn't know I could. I loved the way she interacted with the people at the library. The way she made people feel seen and heard. Always listening. It was how she said she remembered and knew what to recommend for people. She listened, and she asked questions.

I watched her surprise a tentative teen when they came up to check out a book. I had never heard of the title before and wasn't sure I would have read it even if I had. But Ryan instantly started to talk to the girl about the book and how much she had enjoyed it. Ryan then asked the girl what books she would recommend for Ryan based on that book. Then Ryan wrote them down. I watched her look them up. She made me wait while she looked them up in the database. When I asked why she was going to the trouble of looking up the books if she wasn't going to read them, she looked at me like I had grown two heads.

"What makes you think I'm not going to read them? I happen to like that author."

In one of our phone conversations, I asked her if she had seen the girl again. She said she had and that they were talking about starting a reading group for people who liked that genre. Since all the readers Ryan knew who read those books tended to be quiet introverts, it might be fun to get them together to talk about something that they all liked.

"The group wouldn't meet often," she said. "They are introverts, and I don't want to drain their social battery."

Not being an introvert, I wouldn't have thought of that. I would have tried for meetings every week or something. Once a month was what Ryan suggested. It would give them a friend base and also an outlet to talk about the books that not a lot of their classmates read.

I told my mother about Ryan. I told her about all the kind things she does. And we talked about the bullying that she had to put up with, both in high school and at the library. Which got us talking about Tammy.

"I remember that one. I saw her in action on the playground when she was in fifth grade. It was awful. She had a poor girl in tears. But there wasn't anything that you could put a finger on to report. She wasn't aggressive. It was all in her delivery. A slight change of tone, and it was a perfectly normal statement or question. I tried to catch her a few times."

"How did I not know about this? It wasn't a big school?"

"She flew under everyone's radar. Unless you were the one she was picking on."

I described the last time I saw her bothering Ryan. She agreed that it was the same practice as before.

By the time I got home, it was too late to call Ryan. I would have to try to get a hold of her during the day. I wouldn't be able to see her until the following day. The parent-teacher meetings were scheduled to go till eight. It would be late again when I got back to my apartment. Too late to go to her house.

I decided to send her a text in the morning. It was the best I could do short of seeing her.

Chapter 24

Ryan

I rode my motorcycle in the morning. I needed to feel the freedom I felt riding it and feeling the wind blow on my face.

I received a text from Braden before I left.

I can't meet up with you today. Parent-Teacher conferences. I'll try to call you later.

I was disappointed that I wouldn't see him and, at the same time, relieved. I wasn't sure how to face him after the fiasco of our date. I felt so bad. He had planned a beautiful evening for us, and I pretty much brought it to a crashing end.

Annie had given me a pep talk at breakfast. It had helped in the moment, but as I rode my bike to the library, I started to get a feeling of dread. I knew that everything was going to be okay. It was just going to take some patience with myself to make it through the day. Anxiety attacks like the one I had the night before wore me out both physically and mentally.

I followed Annie into work. After stowing my helmet in the building, we walked to the coffee shop from the library parking lot. Frank hadn't shown up yet, and neither of us wanted to be the first ones in that morning.

"Do you really have a safe room in the library?"

"Yes, it isn't like the ones you see in the movies with the steel door and all the supplies. It's just an easily defensible closet."

"You're kidding me? You really do have a plan."

"Of course, I have a plan. When haven't I had a plan? Remember high school? Who had the already set in place scenario for skipping school if we needed to?"

"You did. I thought it was just a fluke. I never put it together that you were so prepared."

"I'm not really. I only think about planning a lot. It is somehow calming to work out all these safety scenarios. Knowing that there is a plan helps me feel safer. I sometimes lie in bed and make plans when I can't sleep."

"You mean the same way I plan how to spend thirty million dollars?"

"You still do that?"

"Oh, yeah. Especially on nights I can't fall asleep. The trick is to try to keep all the numbers in my head. My brain usually gives up and lets me go to sleep. I haven't found a way to spend it all since I can't spend more than a million at one time. The things I buy have to be physical and usable. No buying random mansions."

"That is weirdly specific. No wonder we're friends."

We were laughing when we walked into Connie's place. I went up to the counter to order and pay for our treats. Some days, they had new things to try. It was always a mystery which days. It depended on how much stress Connie was under. The more stress, the more time she spent baking her feelings. I felt bad that I hoped she had been stress-baking that morning.

I was just about to pick something when I noticed someone standing behind me. At first, it startled me. Then I realized that I knew him and relaxed. Owen, Jared's partner at the garden supply, was a laid-back and friendly person. He was also really good-looking. There were a number of women trying to get his attention. Janet said there was a list at the church of the ones trying to get his attention and the odds on whether they would succeed. She said it wasn't gambling exactly, since no money changed hands. The list was updated regularly.

I was surprised that he was alone. Jared was usually with him in the mornings.

"Hey, Ryan. How are things going?"

"Pretty good. Are you eating in?"

"No, I just came in to grab a coffee before I start work." His smile brightened as he looked over my head. "Hello, Connie. Anything new today?"

"Yes, but it all sold out. Do you want your regular?"

"Sure, but I think Ryan was here first."

"That's okay. You go ahead." I moved to let him get in front of me.

"Thanks," he said as he took the cup. "I'm paying for Ryan's, too."

"Thanks, Owen."

"No problem. I'm picking up for Jason, and he's paying, so no big deal."

I laughed as I took my cup and went to our table.

"Anything new?" Annie was setting up her laptop when I got there.

"Nope, and yes."

That got her to look up. "What?"

"Yes, there was something new, and they are all gone."

"Oh, well, that's not fair. I'll see what there is. Be right back."

I was just starting to take a sip when a chair pulled out across from me. I was going to say something when I noticed that it was Connie.

"Here, I set it aside for you." She placed a beautiful cinnamon muffin in front of me.

"This looks yummy." She had placed one at Annie's spot as well. When Annie returned with her coffee, she oohed and awed as well. "What's in it?"

"Cinnamon, obviously, but there is apple pie filling in the center. Like an apple-filled donut, only a muffin."

"Nice." I took a bite and tasted the lovely cinnamon. I was surprised by the filling, even though I knew it would be there. I wasn't expecting it to be so decadent. "I have no idea how you come up with these."

"I'm stressed. That's how." She sounded put out. My mind raced to try to remember if I could be the reason—the perils of having a guilty conscience.

"What happened this time?" Annie was trying to talk around a mouthful of muffin. She gave up, sitting back to enjoy the flavors exploding in her mouth.

"The usual. My mother. I don't want to talk about it." She focused on me. "How are you? How did the date go last night? I want to hear all about it." She looked over at the counter and saw her assistant, Becky, waving at her. "Talk fast. Becky's about to come drag me back."

"Not much to tell. I had a panic attack and didn't even get to try the food."

"Crap. You okay?" She was in the process of getting up, waving at Becky as she did. But she sat back down. I could almost hear Becky's sigh from where we sat.

"I'm fine. I got overstimulated by the new environment and lost it. Braden took me home. I feel so bad. I know that he said everything would be okay. I'm just,"

"Anxious and worried that he isn't going to want to be with you because you have an anxiety attack when you get overstimulated?" Annie rolled her eyes. We had had this conversation the night before and on other occasions.

"Yes."

"I don't think that is going to be a problem." Connie stood up and started moving away from our table. "I wish we weren't so busy this morning. This always happens when I want to sit and take a break. If I wanted to be busy, it would be dead in here."

"We should head to the library. Frank is probably having a fit and trying to get everything ready for the day." I started gathering up my things. I still had most of my muffin left. I put it carefully in my bag.

"The library doesn't open for another hour," Connie said.

"Yup, and Frank is likely panicking, thinking we are dead on the side of the road and not making it in today, leaving him to run the whole show. That is literally what he told us the last time we were late." Annie put air quotes around late.

"Wish me luck." Connie headed for the counter and the now glaring Becky.

"You going to be okay?" Annie nudged me as we made it out to the sidewalk.

"I hope so. I can let you know when we get to the end of the day."

I did not need to wait till the end of the day to decide whether I was going to be okay. Tammy decided that for me within the first hour.

I saw her come through the door just as I went around the corner of the desk to pick up a book I had accidentally pushed off. The light in her eyes reminded me of the look my grandmother's cat would get right before it pounced on its prey.

"Oh, Ryan, I'm so sorry to hear about your date last night. That must have been awful for Braden."

Wow. Just wow. The way she spun it, you would think that Braden had had a panic attack.

"Good morning, Tammy. How can I help you?"

Tammy looked at me with narrowed eyes. This was not going as she planned. I hadn't tried to defend myself or even shrink. I was channeling all the things Kate and I had talked about. Don't acknowledge the comment and stay in control of the narrative. I could do this. Once Tammy left, I would throw up. Until then. I could do this.

"Oh, you must have been so embarrassed. I heard you didn't even get to eat anything. Poor Braden put so much work into the date, and then you messed it up."

"I have the book you were waiting for." I reached under the counter and pulled up the book I had put on hold for her, the one I knew she didn't want.

"I don't need that book anymore."

"Oh, okay. I'll reshelve it later. Was there something that you were looking for then? Or are you just browsing?"

"Are you going out with him again? I hope you didn't scare him off. I heard he was talking to Jackie this morning at the coffee shop before school."

"Oh, were you able to try the new muffins?"

"What?"

"Muffins, the apple pie muffins at the coffee shop. If you were there that early, there should have been some muffins."

"No, I didn't try the muffins. I don't eat those things." The disgust on her face was tinged with something else. I wondered when the last time she had had anything other than black coffee. She had once commented on how she ate carefully. Implying that I did not.

"Well, your loss."

"Are you going out with him again, or did you blow your chances. I heard he has been spending a lot of time with Jackie."

"If there isn't anything I can get for you, can you step aside. Florie is waiting to check out her book." I motioned toward the woman standing behind her.

"I would like to check this out. If you're finished with whatever that was." Florie all but shoved Tammy to the side. She put her book on the counter and then did a hip check on Tammy, who hadn't moved from her spot. With what I think can best be described as a huff, Tammy left the library.

Both Florie and I watched her go. When she turned back to look at me, Florie glanced at my face and asked, "Do you need to throw up now?"

"Yes, and no." I did a quick check of myself. Did I feel like I was going to throw up the wonderful muffin? Yes. Was I going to? No.

"You did good. I'm proud of you. I'm just returning the book." She pointed at the book she had put in front of me. "I was here as backup. I saw her come in and thought you might need help. But, you didn't. You did really well. I'm proud of you. Keep that up, and she might think twice if she can't get a rise out of you." She tapped the desk and turned away.

I watched her chat for a minute with one of the ladies sitting by the new releases. She pointed at a book before walking away. The woman stood and brought the book up to the counter.

"I think you met my granddaughter, her name is Gina. We came in the other week to get a book for her English class."

"I remember you helped me when I panicked the other day with the crowd control."

"You had things under control. I'm glad to see you handling her," she made a gesture toward the door Tammy had gone out of. "She is certainly trouble."

I handed her back her book. "Would you be interested in joining a book club? There's one that meets here once a week. I think you might like the ladies involved."

"That would be lovely, thank you for telling me about it."

"I'll have one of them get in touch with you. Is it okay if I give them your contact info, or would you rather just come to the next meeting?"

"I think I'd just like to come. I don't have a mobile phone, and I try to be outside a lot this time of year. I like sitting in the park."

"That sounds lovely. The next meeting is," —I looked down at the calendar on the desk—"nine tomorrow morning."

"I'll see you then.'

I finished typing her information into the computer and checked out the book for her.

"That went well." I jumped when Annie spoke behind me.

"What went well? "

"Tammy. You handled that well. I was waiting to see if I had to rescue you. I think most of the people here were waiting to see if they needed to rescue you."

"That is not as comforting as you seem to think it is. It kind of makes me feel like everyone thinks I'm weak or something."

"If we thought you couldn't handle it, we would have all said something. Did Kate teach you how to do that?"

"She did. The other day, when I went to visit her during my lunch. I wasn't sure if I was going to be able to do it. I thought I was going to throw up."

"Well, you didn't, and you did great. Any word from Braden today? Other than the text this morning?"

I picked up my phone and looked. He didn't usually text during the morning. If he did, it was always during lunch. There weren't any texts. I felt a little disheartened. Which was stupid since I knew he wouldn't have.

"I wouldn't worry about what she was saying about Jackie. I know for a fact she has a crush on another teacher, up at the school."

"How do you know that?"

"Yoga."

"Yoga? Is that code for some mystical way you have for gathering information?"

"No, you are so weird. I go to yoga on Tuesday evenings, and Jackie is in my yoga class. You would know this if you ever came with me."

"I thought you told Esther you didn't go to the yoga class anymore."

"I don't go to that yoga class. I go to a different one now."

"What else do you learn in yoga?"

"You are coming with me next time. Don't ride your motorcycle next Tuesday. And bring comfortable clothes."

"Am I going to regret this?"

"Probably," Annie smirked as she walked off. I was going to regret this. And I didn't even remember saying I wanted to go. This was how Annie got me to do everything. She just told me I was going. She usually spent a few weeks asking me or setting the stage. When she was ready, she would announce it. I would do what she wanted me to do. Occasionally, I had a good time.

Chapter 25

Ryan

As the afternoon went on, I thought about texting Braden. I had decided that if I didn't hear from him by the time I left the library, I would send him a text. The longer I waited, the more insecure I became about our relationship.

When I checked my phone for what was subjectively the thousandth time, Annie rolled her eyes at me. "Just text the man, you're driving me crazy with all this phone checking."

I opened up our text thread to send him a message when one popped up on the screen.

Sorry, I haven't texted. I've been busy. Don't know how the information got here, but I heard about Tammy from another teacher. This is such a small town. I'm proud of you. I have back-to-back meetings till eight. I'll try to call if I get a chance.

I read it through a few times, trying to decide what to say. Why, why was it so hard to say anything? This was stupid. I wrote the first thing I thought of, *Okay. I'll talk to you later or tomorrow.* I hit send before I could overthink it. Then I started to overthink it.

"What did he say?"

"He said that he was in meetings all evening and that he'd talk to me tomorrow. Also, he heard about Tammy, and he was proud of me." I didn't feel like it was such a big deal. If anything, I had been overthinking everything. The only thing I kept saying to myself was that it shouldn't be such a surprise to people that I could stand up for myself.

"What did you say?"

"Okay, talk to you tomorrow."

"That's it? No romantic thoughts for the man?"

"No, should I have? Oh my gosh, I should have said something." I put my head down on the desk.

Frank took that moment to pop out of his office. He had been hiding in there all day. He made occasional appearances before scurrying back in and shutting the door.

"What time are you finishing up here today?" He pointed at the clock. It was a few minutes past closing, and we hadn't done anything.

"We're on it." We both hurried around, shutting off the computers and closing and locking the doors.

Mabel made an appearance before we had finished. "You riding your motorcycle home? You'd better leave soon. Before it gets dark."

"You go on and leave," Annie said.

"You go, we got this," Frank joined in.

"Okay." I gathered my things and headed out the back door. I would be lucky to get home before it started getting dark.

I was getting on my bike when Kate came out and headed toward her car.

"Hello!" She waved at me as she put her things into the front seat. I rode over to where she was standing.

"Hello, heading home?"

"I am. It has been a long day. You?" She stood up from putting things in her back seat.

"I am as well."

" I wanted to talk to you at some point. Things to tell you." Kate looked troubled. "Did you want to follow me home? We could talk there."

"I need to get home before it gets dark. Why don't you follow me home? I can feed us dinner, and we can talk."

"That sounds great. Thanks."

"Do you remember the way, or did you want to follow me?"

"I think I can make it. I'll see you in a few."

I nodded and rode off. I was thinking about what to feed her when I pulled into my driveway. As I went past the house, I saw something on the step outside the door. I hurried through parking and closing up the garage. I rarely get packages on the doorstep. I usually don't order anything big enough that they couldn't put in the mailbox.

Kate was just pulling up to the house when I bent to pick up the brown paper-covered package. As I lifted it, I realized it was open at the top. Careful not to drop it, I looked in and saw the most beautiful flowers.

I opened the door, balancing my things and the beautiful flowers. Kate came up behind me and held the door.

"Those are beautiful. Who are they from?"

"I don't know." Putting everything down, I opened the paper on the flowers. They were beautifully arranged in a vase with a card tucked inside. I carefully took the card and opened it.

Thinking about you. I'll call you tomorrow. Braden

"Again, wow. I think your date went well."

I felt my face heat up. "I guess it did."

I placed the flowers in the middle of the table so they would be the first thing I saw when I walked into the room. Between my study and the kitchen, it was a toss-up as to which room I spent more time in.

"Let's get dinner started, and we can talk." I opened the freezer and took out the first meal I came to. "It looks like we are having lasagna tonight. Janet and Rose don't trust me to cook for myself, so they periodically sneak in and fill my freezer. I am the luckiest of nieces."

I looked at the directions and turned on the oven. I didn't wait till the oven preheated and put the casserole dish in. I set the timer and went to sit down at the table.

"You aren't going to wait for it to preheat. I had that drummed into me while I was growing up. Wait till the oven is hot."

"Nope. I never do. I just give the timer a little more time. If I were making something from scratch, I would turn it on and let it preheat." I opened the cupboard and took out a glass. I looked at Kate and motioned to the glass. "I have water, juice, and I think root beer."

"Water is fine."

I filled two glasses and sat down at the table. Kate moved her glass around in front of her.

"Are you okay, Kate?"

"The board let me know that the pastor has decided to retire. And they are starting the search process. I like it here. I want to stick around and work with this congregation. There is so much life here. I have a feeling that they are going to look for someone else."

"Who told you this?"

"Steve Philips. He's the head of the search committee that brought me here. I think he was outvoted on it. He has not been thrilled with having a female pastor."

"Janet told me about that. He was the only one to vote against you being here. Did you put your name in for consideration?"

"Mr. Phillips made it sound as though they were not going to accept my application. To not bother."

"Did you put your name on the list?"

"Of course. That was what Janet and I were talking about last night. She told me that he was the only one who didn't want me. And that he said all that because if I don't put my name in, then they can't vote for me."

"From what I know of him, that seems possible. He is not big on change, and for him, having a woman as a pastor is a very big change. I think having you here is good for the town."

"Not everyone in town goes to this church."

"True. Janet said that since you started here, the congregation has grown. A lot."

"It has. That scares me a lot. What if I mess up? I'm not as experienced as I would like to be. And at the same time, I know I can do this. It's very confusing."

"So, what you're struggling with is confidence?"

"If you succeed at something, then people expect more from you. And what if I don't have more?"

"What do you mean?"

"What if people keep coming to the church, and what I have to offer isn't enough after a while?"

I looked at her and waited for what she was saying to sink in. Wasn't this exactly what I struggle with all the time? Isn't it why I never try to step outside of my comfortable life? Other than the fact that I have anxiety attacks, why don't I try to do more?

"I understand. I don't think your problem is as big as you are thinking. Are you going to be doing anything different from what you're doing now? Other than finally putting up decor in your office? I feel overwhelmed every time I try to do something new. My therapist told me that it wasn't that I couldn't do the things, but I let the anxiety tell me what was impossible."

"I know that what I am doing isn't going to change in theory. Everywhere I've been, I always knew I was temporary. This feels different."

"That's because it is different. You'll get to stick around and hopefully grow old with us."

"So, what you're saying is that I am blowing this all out of proportion."

"Not out of proportion. It is scary. But I also know that you are more than capable. Besides, you have the book club as backup."

We both laughed at that last thought. The timer went off on the oven, announcing our dinner. The rest of the evening was spent talking about funny stories from her other congregations.

As I lay in bed thinking about the day, I thought about what I had said to Kate. How much of my life do I spend in fear? Fear of Tammy. Fear of change. I decided to look into finding a therapist to help me with the next step in my journey. I would check the weather in the morning and ride in. I would finally get my time at the park to do some thinking and use the public wifi to find a new therapist. The park, oddly enough, was the most private place I could think of to do it. No one would be looking over my shoulder or trying to find out what I was doing.

It would be private to do it here. But at the park, I didn't have to worry about anyone coming by. My family knew my schedule and knew that I would go in late tomorrow. If I were here, people would stop by to visit. The park would be the best place for privacy.

As I was starting to drift off, my phone rang. I answered it, but I don't remember who it was that called.

Chapter 26

Braden

I called Ryan the night before. She was half asleep, so we only talked for a few minutes. I knew she still felt uncomfortable with how the date had ended. I also knew that the longer we went before seeing each other, the more awkward she would feel and the more she would overthink the entire thing.

I sent the flowers to let her know that I was still interested in her. I was worried that she would pull back from me after the date. I needed her to know that I cared. I didn't say that on the note. I debated with signing it, *Love, Braden*.

She said she only worked in the afternoon, filling in for someone. It was usually her day off, but she owed them a favor. I couldn't remember if it was Annie or someone else. I was planning to go by after school let out. I wanted to spend time with her. I missed her. The realization I had the other night about my feelings had me walking pretty high in the clouds. Even if I hadn't told her.

I had made it through the first hour of school when Stan came into the room. His hair was standing up, and his face was red from running.

"Is she okay? Have you heard what hospital they took her to?"

"What are you talking about?"

"Ryan! She was in an accident. Some of my students saw her motorcycle and the ambulance pulling away. They said it looked bad."

"When did this happen?" My heart had stopped beating. And then it started back up, but at twice the pace.

I pulled my phone out and hit the speed dial for Ryan's phone. It went directly to voicemail. I tried Annie's number. Ryan had texted it to me if I needed to get a hold of her, and she wasn't answering her phone at work. I questioned why I would need to get in touch with her that quickly, but I put the number into my phone. I texted her first, before I called, so she would know it was me calling.

"Hello, Braden, why are you calling me?"

"Hello, Annie. Have you heard about Ryan? How is she? Are you with her?"

"What? What do you mean, how's Ryan?"

"The accident. This morning. Her motorcycle." I wasn't speaking in complete sentences. I knew I wasn't. I couldn't think clearly enough for anything to form.

"I have no idea what you're talking about. Ryan was in an accident?"

"That was what I said. Someone saw her being put into an ambulance this morning on their way to school. I just found out."

"Wait. Let me check. I'm not at the library. I need to call Janet."

She hung up on me before I could say anything. I started packing up my bag. I couldn't stay at the school. I needed to get ready to leave. If she needed me, I would go wherever she was.

My phone rang as I started to leave the room. The students had started filling up the room. I told the students someone would be in in a few minutes. I looked around and made a decision.

"Gina, you and Gil are in charge until another teacher arrives." They both nodded and then started to organize the students into discussion groups so they could talk about their books. The groups were organized by the genre they read. An idea I got from talking to Ryan about her reading groups.

I hit the accept button and put the phone to my ear. "Annie?"

"Janet hasn't heard anything. She knows that they would have called either her or me since we are on the emergency card Ryan carries with her. Are you sure it was Ryan who was in the accident?"

"I'm not sure of anything. Stan came in and told me that he was told she was in an accident. That someone saw her leave in the ambulance." I pushed my hand through my hair. I almost ran over a student on my way to the main office. "Can I call you back? I need to get someone to cover my classes." I didn't wait to hear what she said before I pushed the end call button.

I walked into the office and headed straight for Mrs. Tussle's desk. She didn't look like she was in a good mood, which was fine; I wasn't either.

"Mrs. Tussle, I need to leave. A family emergency just came up, and I need to leave. I have a class getting ready to start, and someone needs to be in there. I don't have the time to find someone myself."

"I can go in for you, this is my off period." I turned to see Jackie standing in the doorway. "Stan just told me. I can cover for you. I'll see who I can find to cover the other classes until or if they find a substitute."

"You teach Math. What do you know about English?" Mrs. Tussle snapped at Jackie with her best disapproving glare to top it off.

"Well, I speak English, and I can read and write. I am pretty sure that should cover it for the one hour." She turned to me, "Do you have any plans for today or things that people need to do?"

"No, we were going to discuss the books they are reading outside of class. And try to get others interested in their book. I put two of the students in charge. They have divided up into their discussion groups." I started past her and touched her shoulder on my way by. "Thank you." I moved quickly out the door. I could hear Jackie and Mrs. Tussle talking.

"Well, Mrs. Tussle, what hour do you have free. I bet you have a book you want to interest the kids in."

I didn't know Jackie had it in her to go toe to toe with Tussle. She had some serious skills. If I was reading the signs right, she was trying to get to know Stan. I could probably help with that.

I decided to run to the library. It would take me longer to get my car and then drive the three blocks to the library. I dodged pedestrians as I hurried down the sidewalk. I tried not to let my bag hit anyone as I went past. I might have almost hit a small child as I ran.

I looked back and saw a boy in a dinosaur costume walking with someone I assumed was his mother, though you could never tell.

I made it up the steps to the library only to be met with a locked door. I pounded on it, but no one answered.

"Braden!" I turned to see Annie hurrying up the sidewalk from the direction of the coffee shop. I forgot that was where she usually went in the mornings. I would have to remember and see if I could meet up with Ryan before school some days. Ryan, my heart caught in my chest when I thought of her.

"Braden, I'm glad I found you. I tried to call you back, but you didn't answer. Janet is trying to reach the surrounding hospitals. She is also calling the University Hospital to see if they took her there. It's so far away that the only way she would get there is by helicopter. The local hospital should know if they sent her out from there. Janet is on the list of people they can talk to, so at least she can get answers. Let me open the door."

I moved out of the way to give her access to the lock. I noticed someone hurrying towards the library from the corner of my eye. Annie grabbed my arm and practically shoved me into the library. She hurried in behind me. Sticking her head out of the door, she yelled, "We are not open yet." Before slamming the door and relocking it.

"You would think we were Target on Black Friday the way people try to get in here early. Okay,"—she put her things down and picked up a phone—"I'll call a few places, and you get on the computer and see if the local paper has put anything out there.

I turned on the computer and started looking for the website. On the banner for the day was an article about a motorcycle accident. My heart fell the rest of the way to my feet.

A young woman motorcyclist was injured in a collision. She suffered serious injuries and was taken to the hospital. No name was released.

There was a picture of the motorcycle, or what was left of it. It looked like Ryan's bike. I just couldn't be sure.

"Annie, is this Ryan's motorcycle?"

Annie came over to the computer and looked. She enlarged the picture. I looked away. If there was any blood on the ground or any other sign of Ryan being injured, I didn't want to see it. I didn't think my heart could take it.

"That," Annie sighed as she leaned away from me, "is not Ryan's bike. It's the wrong type. That's a Harley. Ryan does *not* ride a Harley."

I felt tears start to slide down my face. The relief almost choking me. I had to put my head down.

"It isn't her. Oh my gosh. I think I'm going to throw up." Annie raced away from the desk, heading for the restrooms. I knew exactly how she felt.

There was a pounding on the front door. A voice was yelling something I couldn't quite make out. The closer I got to the door I could understand some of what was being said. I moved the shade over the window and saw Janet standing at the door.

I opened the lock and let her in, careful not to let anyone else in. There was a cry of "Hey!" as I relocked the door.

"I couldn't find out anything. No one would talk to me at the hospital or the police department. I don't know what to do next. I..."

I cut her off before she could say anything else. "It wasn't her. That wasn't her on the motorcycle. We looked it up online. At the newspaper. There was a picture. It wasn't her."

"Oh my," Janet placed a hand on her heart and sank into the nearest chair. "It was like reliving her mother's accident all over again. I think I aged ten years. I don't ever want to feel that again." She burst into tears. I leaned down and wrapped an arm around her. She stood up, almost knocking me over, and wrapped her arms around me in a fierce hug. I felt each shudder of her body as the tears of relief flowed.

I needed to call people and let them know. So many people were worried. Annie came back from the restroom. Seeing Janet, she joined in on the hug. I was now enveloped in a group hug. I don't think I have ever had a group hug before.

The front door opened, and we all broke apart to turn and see who was coming in.

"Back, you jackals. The library isn't open yet." He slammed the door in the face of someone trying to get in. "I swear the book club is getting more aggressive each day."

"Oh my. They were out trying to find Ryan." Janet pushed Frank out of the way and opened the door.

"I just told them they couldn't come in yet. What are you doing?" Frank tried to stop her, but it was a losing battle.

"Someone was in an accident this morning—a bad motorcycle accident. Up until a few minutes ago, we thought it was Ryan."

"Are you sure she's safe?" Frank's complexion had gone several shades whiter in the few seconds it took for the information to sink in. "I need to sit down."

The group outside the door made it in past Janet. She did slam the door in someone's face. Because I could hear someone yelling about unfairness and favoritism. That got someone in the group mad because they turned and headed back towards the door.

"Florie, stop. Just let him be. You know he gets upset over everything. He must have noticed the commotion and wanted to get in on it." Florie turned and walked over towards Annie.

"Sweetie, how can we help? Do we know anything, yet?"

"It wasn't her. It wasn't Ryan."

"Oh, thank heavens." Florie reached over to another woman and started hugging her.

"If it wasn't Ryan, then who was it?" One of the others asked.

"I don't know, but we'd better find out. That family is going to need some support."

"Does Kate know? I know she and Ryan are getting to be good friends. Did anyone tell her Ryan was in an accident?"

I could hear footsteps hurrying from the back of the library. Everyone else turned toward the sound.

"Is that you, Mabel?"

"Yes, of course it's me. Who else comes in that door?" She hurried toward us, practically dragging someone with her. I wondered if she was Kate. I thought it might be. Ryan had mentioned she was the pastor next door. "Kate said it wasn't Ryan in the accident. It was someone else."

"We just found that out. Janet just told us."

"Braden told me," Janet said.

"Does anyone know where Ryan could be? She isn't answering her phone, either the one at home or her cell. She usually answers when one of us calls."

"I saw her." All eyes turned toward Kate.

"Where?" I was already heading for the door.

"She was in the park when I last saw her," Katherine said.

I hurried out the door. I took a right when I reached the sidewalk. I tried to keep my pace at a normal walk. She was okay. She wasn't in the hospital. Everything was going to be okay. I kept repeating that to myself as I walked.

I pulled out my phone and called Stan. He would get the word out to people at the school. I would probably feel foolish for rushing out the way I did when everything calmed down. Well, maybe not. I was pretty scared.

"Hello, Stan. This is Braden. It wasn't Ryan in the accident. We don't know who it was, but it wasn't Ryan. Let everyone know. I'll talk to you later." I hung up after leaving the message. I was glad it was only a message. I wasn't ready to talk to anyone yet. I needed to see Ryan. I needed to make sure for myself that she was okay.

I stepped onto the grass of the park, looking around at the benches. There was no sign of Ryan. I moved farther into the park. The closer I came to the bandstand on the far side of the park, the more my heart sank. I couldn't find her. I needed to see her.

As I rounded the bandstand, I saw her. She was sitting on the steps.

"Hey, Braden, what are you doing here? Don't you have school?"

I didn't say anything; I couldn't say anything. I dropped down onto the seat next to her and wrapped my arms around her and held her against me. The relief that flooded my body as I felt her against me was more than I could hold inside my chest, and all the emotions started to leak out of my eyes. When she wrapped her arms around me, saying my name, I lost all the restraint I had and let the tears flow freely down my cheek. I had never felt so scared and then so relieved in my life. I never wanted to go through that again.

Chapter 27

Ryan

"Braden, are you okay? What happened?" I tightly wrapped my arms around him. I couldn't think of anything that could have happened that would cause this kind of reaction.

He pulled away from me just far enough to look me in the eyes. "Did you ride your motorcycle this morning?"

"No, I'm working for Annie this afternoon, and then I have a meeting with some kids who want to start a book club. It would be too late for me to ride home. Why? What happened?"

He didn't say anything; he kept looking at my eyes and stroking my cheek with his fingertips. "We thought you were in an accident. Some of the kids at school saw a young woman being put into an ambulance and thought it was you. I have never been so scared in my life."

He buried his face into my neck. When he lifted his head, he pressed his forehead to mine. His cheeks were wet with tears. I reached up and wiped them carefully from his face.

"I thought I lost you. I thought I wouldn't get to tell you that I was falling in love with you. That I have been falling in love with since high school. And that it only took seeing you in your tank at that pull-off to light the fire again. I am falling in love with your smile, your tears, your fears, the clumsy way you try to talk to people when you're nervous. And the way you are standing up for yourself." He stroked my face and then gently pressed his lips to mine. I tried to press a little firmer into his lips, but he pulled back.

"I think I'm falling in love with you, too," I said.

Then he did kiss me. I held on tightly to his shoulders, afraid to let go. When he stopped kissing me, he pulled me as close to him as he could and rested his head on mine. We sat like that, holding each other quietly, watching the people move around us, completely unaware of how my world had just shifted.

"Why are you here?" Braden's voice was husky and a little raspy from the crying. "No one knew where you were until Kate came into the library with someone named Mabel."

"Mabel is the children's librarian. She's been at the library longer than anyone."

"When Stan came into my room and said that he had heard you had been in an accident, I thought my heart was going to stop. I think it did for a minute. I have never been so scared. I even stood up to Ms.Tussle. I told her I was leaving and just took off."

"Wow, I would never have been able to stand up to her. She terrified me back when we were at the school, and she still scares me when she comes into the library. Though if you want to see something cute, you should see her when she gets around Frank. That is, unless Marge is there, then she is quiet and in and out the door fast."

"I want you to know that I was not embarrassed the other night. Your panic attack is not anything that I would ever be embarrassed by. It is a part of who you are. And I am falling in love with every part of you. I am not going anywhere."

"I talked about the anxiety and fear with Kate this morning. I think it's time I start to work on new coping strategies. I want to try new things. I'm tired of being stuck with the same things all the time. Only familiar places and familiar people. There are probably some things that I will always struggle with, but I want to try new things. Slowly. Not everything all at once."

"Do you have a pan?"

"I've been reaching out to therapists. Maybe I can find someone who can help me."

"That sounds like a good plan. I want to be a part of that plan. If you'll let me." He pulled me tighter against him. I could still feel him tremble a little as the fear and adrenaline left his body. That feeling of coming down from fear was something I was very aware of.

"Are you okay?"

"I will be. Is this what you feel like after you have an anxiety attack?"

"Sort of. I think it's very similar."

"I think we should get you to the library. Everyone there would probably like to see you after the scare I put everyone through. I may have called Annie. Who then called your aunt. Who then called everyone else. I am pretty sure I scared a few years off of Frank." He kissed my temple.

"I guess we should probably go then. I am confused about something. Didn't anyone see my car behind the library?"

"I don't think anyone thought to look there. I know I didn't. The weather is beautiful, and I assumed you rode in."

"I was going to, but since I was working later, I decided to drive in to work. Kate saw me, though. We talked. I told her I was going to be here and what my plan was."

"That was probably why she rushed in like she did. We were all trying to come up with where you could be when she came in and said you were here. I rushed out of the library so fast I don't know what anyone else did."

"We should probably head back then."

I tried to disentangle myself from his arms so I could get my things together. He only tightened his hold.

"I know we need to go and let everyone know that you are fine. I just need another minute with you. I'm not ready to let go."

As it turned out, we didn't need to go anywhere. They came to us. I saw my aunts, and Annie headed for us, and I braced for impact.

Annie practically fell on us.

"Let her go. You had your turn." She wrapped her arms so tight around me that Braden had no choice but to let go. "Do not scare us like that again."

"In my defence," I choked out. "I didn't do anything. Other people jumped to the conclusion that it was me."

"Doesn't matter. I was scared to death after Braden called, and no one could reach you. Why didn't you answer your phone?"

"I forgot to charge it last night and ran the battery dead looking for a therapist. "

"While I commend your choice of getting a therapist. I am going to invest in one of those portable chargers so this doesn't happen again."

When she finally let me go, I stood up. Braden had already gathered my things and was waiting for me. I was about to suggest that we head back to the library when my aunts grabbed me. Both of them at the same time.

"I thought it was just like your mother all over again. I don't think I can do that.'

"I will do everything I can to make sure you don't have to go through that again. I promise."

"Good," Janet said.

"Remember that," Rose squeezed me even harder. "Frank is back at the library holding down the fort. The book club is helping him sort through the crowd that showed up. Everyone who drove by the accident thought it was you, and they are trying to set eyes on you to make sure you're safe. You'd better plan on coming into the library now. The number of people trying to talk to you after the bee is nothing compared to the number of people who have already stopped by to make sure you're okay."

"Who was in the accident," I asked as I tried to take my things from Braden. He resolutely held on to them.

"A young woman from out of state. She is going to be okay. What Florie was able to find out, which isn't much, is that she is hurt but not as bad as we feared. Someone is getting in touch with the chaplain at the hospital to help with any family that needs to come in."

Of course, Janet had everything under control as far as helping out. She was in her element. If Annie was impressed with my planning skills, it is nothing compared to how quickly Janet can get things moving.

The library was in controlled chaos when we walked through the door. Frank was fielding questions and trying to get people to move away from his desk and find somewhere else to loiter.

"She is fine. It wasn't her. She was just down at the park." Janet had assumed command.

Marge came through the door just after us. She grabbed me up in a hug just as everyone else had. "Don't you scare my Frank like that ever again, young lady."

It was hard for her to sound harsh when she was wearing such a large smile.

The biggest surprise was Connie. She came into the library looking as harried as everyone else. I was so surprised that so many people were worried about me. I knew that I was known, but not that I was this cared for. I guess I needed to work on my feelings of self-worth along with the anxiety.

Behind Connie was Owen. He stayed close to her. I thought I saw him reach out to her a few times. But lowered his hand quickly, before she noticed.

"Ryan, Oh my gosh. Are you okay? Someone came in and said they thought they saw you being put in an ambulance, and then someone else said they saw Braden and Annie both running towards the library."

"I'm fine. It was a case of mistaken identity." I turned to Braden, "How did you know it wasn't me?"

"Annie. She looked at the motorcycle from the one picture the paper had put on their website."

"It was a Harley. You don't ride a Harley." Annie had sat down and was removing her emergency stash of chocolate from her drawer.

"Here, try this instead." Connie handed her a treat from the bag she took from Owen.

"What about me?"

"You get this." Connie grabbed me in a hug. I was going to be covered in bruises from all the tight hugs I was getting.

By the time everyone had settled down and left. I was exhausted. Braden had gone back to the school with the promise of coming back as soon as classes were over.

Chapter 28

Ryan

The phone was ringing as I walked into the house. I put all my bags down on the counter and answered the phone.

"Hello."

"Hello, how was the drive home?"

"Braden, I just saw you." I looked at my watch. "An hour ago."

"What took you so long to get home?"

I leaned against the counter and thought about the last hour. "I went to see my mom."

I had gone right after work. It had been so long since I visited her grave. I always thought it was silly when I was growing up. She wasn't there. Why do I have to go and visit someone who isn't there? For weeks after the woman was in the motorcycle accident, the thought of visiting my mother wouldn't leave my mind. It was something Janet had said that day. *I thought it was your mother all over again.* I remember that day. I remember the absolute loss that engulfed me.

Today I decided to go. To visit her grave and talk to her. I stood there in the rain and cried. I didn't say anything, I just cried. I cried for her and for all I missed with her. All the tears I held onto for so long. When I climbed into the car, I felt a little lighter. A little more sure.

"Hey, Braden."

"Yes."

"I love you."

There was silence on the phone, then I heard him take a deep breath. "Ryan."

"Yes."

"I love you, too."

I felt light swallow me. A smile so big I thought it would crack my face bloomed on my lips. I leaned against the counter. "I wish you were here right now, so I could kiss you."

"Open the door. It's raining out here."

I turned toward the door and unlocked it. As I pulled it open, I found Braden leaning against the wall. Trying to huddle under the small roof over the small stoop.

"What was that you said about a kiss?"

I dropped the receiver and heard it bounce on the floor. I pulled him into the house, pressing my lips against his as soon as he was close enough.

When we finally came up for air, he pressed his forehead to mine. He had told me that it was how he could prolong the closeness of the kiss and breathe, that he wasn't ready to stop touching, and this was the next best thing to kissing for him.

I picked up the phone and put it back on the hook. After closing and locking the door, he took me by the hand and led me down the hall to my study. He sat in my comfy chair and pulled me down onto his lap.

"I know that technically we have only been dating for a short time. But I feel like I have known you all my life. When I saw you ride away from me at the pull-off, I felt like a light that had been put on dim was turned brighter than it had ever been. I knew that being with you was my one goal. My one objective in life. That doesn't sound as romantic as it feels. Ryan, I don't ever want to be away from you. I don't know if this is too soon, but will you marry me?"

"It is soon. And you're right, it does feel like I've known you all my life. Though I think you've at least known of me longer." I stopped talking and leaned into him, putting my head on his shoulder. "Yes."

SIX MONTHS LATER

"ARE YOU SURE THIS IS what you want?"

"Yes, I told you. I want you to be happy and not panicking. If we did this the traditional way, you would be freaking out the entire day and not be comfortable and enjoy yourself."

He was right. I would be panicking. The thought of being surrounded by a lot of people, even though I knew all of them, would be more than I would want to endure. Which is why we found ourselves at the town clerk's office getting the required paperwork.

We had been planning this for a few weeks and, therefore, had all the time to get the right forms and waiting times taken care of.

On that beautiful rainy day when Braden asked me to marry him, I thought it would be farther in the future. Since that day, we have grown closer than I thought I would ever be with anyone.

And here we are, getting our forms and then hurrying down to see Kate, who had agreed to do this for us. We paused just inside the doors of the church. I hadn't told anyone. Except Annie. And my aunts. That was it. Braden had told his mother and his grandparents. Which brought up the question, if you tell people, are you in fact eloping?

It didn't matter. Everything was going to be fine. We were moving into my house that afternoon and possibly having a family cookout. I wasn't in charge of that part. We discovered that the less I was actually in charge of things, the less anxiety I had to deal with. We put the most organized of organizers in charge of the after-elopement party, my aunt Janet.

"Are you ready?"

Was I ready? I felt ready. I did a quick check of what I was feeling. We had been working on my understanding of normal nervousness and anxiety in therapy. I had found a wonderful woman who had helped me understand so much about how my anxiety works. This was normal nervousness. I was going to say I do. I was going to marry someone who made my heart feel safe and treasured. When we kissed, I felt surrounded by warmth and peace, passion and fire. I was ready.

"Yes, I am very ready."

"I'm going to leave you here and take my place. See you in a few minutes." He kissed my cheek before walking off. Kate had shown us where to go and where Braden would stand. Even though it was supposed to just be us, we wanted it to be as close to a regular church wedding as we could get.

Kate had gotten someone to come in and play the piano for us, so I could walk into the chapel with music. When I heard the piano start, I opened the door. My uncle stood on the other side of the door.

"I know it isn't exactly what you had planned, but I didn't want you to walk down the aisle alone." He held out his elbow for me to hold.

"Thank you," I whispered.

"Don't cry. You'll make me cry. Which will get your aunts crying, and then we're all finished."

I looked at the people in the pews. My aunts and cousins were sitting there. As well as Connie. I looked for Annie in the pews.

Annie stepped out from behind my uncle and handed me some flowers. I had forgotten the flowers.

"I'll start you off. You promised me when we were in sixth grade that I would be your maid of honor. I am not going to let you break that promise." She turned and slowly started walking down the aisle.

I looked to the front of the church. Kate was standing at the front, smiling at me. Next to her was Braden. Somewhere between when he left and when he got to the front, he had put on a suit jacket. Next to him was his friend Stan.

Braden's eyes met mine. We didn't break eye contact the entire time I walked toward him. The closer I got to him, the more I felt my heart grow in my chest. I thought I was going to pass out from the love that I was feeling. I had never felt so seen and loved.

My uncle placed my hand in Braden's. As soon as my hand was there, he closed his fingers around it. He gently squeezed, and with that squeeze, I remembered what he had said to me the night before.

"I will never let go. You are the best thing that has ever happened in my life. Ever since you rode into the parking lot when you were sixteen, totally oblivious to the chaos you created, I knew what I wanted in life. Thanks to a bee, I get to have you with me, always.

I didn't hear anything Kate said. I could only look at Braden. I had been looking at him for months. I had stared at him across tables and while we walked and held hands. I had stared at him while he was reading and while we cooked together. But at the moment he said, "I do," all I saw was my future. And it looked really good.

Don't miss out!

Visit the website below and you can sign up to receive emails whenever Elle White publishes a new book. There's no charge and no obligation.

https://books2read.com/r/B-A-DBXFF-ZDLCJ

About the Author

Elle lives in Vermont with her husband and two cats. She spends an inordinate amount of time reading, daydreaming, and writing.

Read more at ellwhiteauthor.com.

www.ingramcontent.com/pod-product-compliance
Lightning Source LLC
LaVergne TN
LVHW090606110826
845146LV00001B/274

* 9 7 9 8 9 9 4 4 7 1 7 1 5 *